…ow, are we doing the ground rules before or after I get my orgasm?'

'Before,' Kate said, any thought of backing away from their agreement obliterated by the heat of his words, the wild rush of desire that bolted through her.

'Then let's do it fast. Before I explode.'

The air was thick with lust as she guided him to the dining table, handed him the pages she'd prepared for their signatures.

'So we're—what?' he asked. 'Signing a contract?'

She nodded. 'With a contract we'll both know where we stand, what we can expect. It keeps things uncomplicated.'

Scott laughed, but didn't refuse, so Kate started running through the clauses. She didn't even make it through the first one before Scott cut her off.

'Katie—you want a contract, then a contract it is. But it's a sex contract—not a prenup or a business merger. And it's not even legally enforceable, as we both know. So can you just give me the basics? Then I'll sign—there's no wa⎯⎯⎯ and we can move on to imp⎯⎯⎯ much lon⎯⎯⎯ to go ins⎯

SYDNEY'S MOST ELIGIBLE...

The men everyone *is talking about!*

Young, rich and gorgeous, Rob, Scott, Brodie
and Luke have the world at their feet
and women queuing to get between their sheets.

Find out how the past and the present collide for them
in this stylish, sexy and glamorous new quartet!

These sexy Sydney tycoons didn't get to the top by
taking the easy way—the only thing they love more
than a challenge is a woman who knows her mind!

So let the fireworks begin...!

HER BOSS BY DAY...
by Joss Wood
Available January 2015

THE MILLIONAIRE'S PROPOSITION
by Avril Tremayne
Available February 2015

THE TYCOON'S STOWAWAY
by Stefanie London
Available March 2015

THE HOTEL MAGNATE'S DEMAND
by Jennifer Rae
Available April 2015

You won't want to miss any of the fabulous books
in this sizzling mini-series!

THE MILLIONAIRE'S PROPOSITION

BY
AVRIL TREMAYNE

Published in Great Britain 2015
by Mills & Boon, an imprint of Harlequin (UK) Limited,
Eton House, 18-24 Paradise Road, Richmond, Surrey, TW9 1SR

© 2015 Harlequin Books S.A.

Special thanks and acknowledgement are given to Avril Tremayne
for her contribution to the *Sydney's Most Eligible...* series.

ISBN: 978-0-263-24842-5

Avril Tremayne is happily settled in her hometown of Sydney, Australia, where her husband and daughter try to keep her out of trouble—not always successfully. When she's not writing or reading she can generally be found eating—although she does *not* cook!

Check out her website: www.avriltremayne.com. Or follow her on Twitter: @AvrilTremayne and Facebook: www.facebook.com/avril.tremayne

Other titles by Avril Tremayne:

HERE COMES THE BRIDESMAID
FROM FLING TO FOREVER
TURNING THE GOOD GIRL BAD

For Peter Alati—best brother ever.

CHAPTER ONE

SCOTT KNIGHT TOOK one look at the redhead standing over at the punchbowl and almost swallowed his tongue.

Tall, confident, beautiful…and dyspeptically cynical, judging by the look on her face. He liked every single thing in that package.

So…exactly what *was* the pick-up etiquette associated with divorce parties? Were they like funerals—no hitting on attendees unless you wanted to look like a slimeball?

He pondered that while he took another look at the redhead.

Strictly speaking, of course, this was a little more than a divorce party; it was a celebratory segue to Willa's new committed relationship with Rob. Scott wouldn't normally have advocated a jump from one hot pan right into another—even when the guy in the second pan was Rob, who was several thousand light years ahead of Willa's ex, Wayne-the-Pain—but he was suddenly cool with it if it lifted the party out of the funereal stakes and opened the way…

The redhead turned to the punchbowl for another dip. Scott noted that her body was divine. And he stopped worrying about anything other than getting his hands on it.

He headed over to the punchbowl with great purpose, grabbing a beer on the way—punch being way too girly for him. 'What's that quote about divorce…?' he asked, tilting his head towards her—but it was a rhetorical question.

She turned before the words had finished leaving his mouth and a slap of undiluted lust walloped him. She was even better close-up. A scorching mix of opulent looks, with slanted grey eyes, wickedly arched dark auburn brows, regal cheekbones…and a top-lip-heavy mouth painted blistering red.

She didn't bother answering. Clearly knew she didn't have

to. Knew he was already caught. He could tell by the way she waited, all self-possessed confidence, for him to continue, with the mere hint of a smile on her insanely sexy lips.

'Jean Kerr, it was,' he continued. '"A lawyer is never entirely comfortable with a friendly divorce, any more than a good mortician wants to finish his job and then have the patient sit up on the table."'

The sexy lips parted in surprise…and then the corners tilted up, just a little. She looked fascinated. He took that as a sign—a *good* sign—that his opening conversational gambit had hit the mark. She was with him. *Yes!*

She took a slow sip of her punch and examined him. Down, up. 'Are you in the market?' she asked, and the smokiness of her voice had his libido purring like a tomcat on the hunt.

Mmm-hmm. She'd not only caught him, she was well on the way to hog-tying him and dumping him in a babbling heap at her feet. And he wasn't complaining.

Scott gave her his *I am available for sex immediately* smile, which he liked to call his Number One smile, because it seemed to be the one that got the most use.

'Why, yes, I do happen to be in the market,' he said.

She laughed. Throatily gorgeous. 'I meant the divorce market.'

'I'm not married, if that's what you're asking. Or engaged.' Little step closer. 'Or partnered in any way, shape or form.'

She made a little moue with her luscious lips. 'Shame. Would have been fun.'

Scott wasn't often taken by surprise, but Cool-Hand Red had managed it with five little words. Why was his singledom a shame? Did she only do married guys?

'Still could be,' he said, rallying fast as he figured that simply couldn't be true. 'Fun, I mean.'

'With no money involved?' Little regretful sigh. 'I don't think so.'

What the *hell*? She not only preferred married men, but they had to *pay*? This was *so* not Willa's scene. It wasn't *his* scene either, and he'd thought he was up for most things—

except for all that hardcore S&M business. Inflicting pain—
and receiving it—thank you but no! Not his cup of tea.

She put down her punch, reached into the small and spar-
kly emerald-green evening bag draped via a chain over her
shoulder, took out an elegant silver card case, flicked it open
one-handed and handed him a plain, crisp white business card.

'"Kate Cleary",' he read. And then, 'Oh…' *Wince.* 'Ouch.'

Another of those throaty laughs. 'Divorce lawyer. Willa's,
in fact. And she's not only sitting up on the mortician's table,
she's leaping off it and twirling across the floor with a dance
partner. And I'm *very* comfortable with that. Now…what's
that *other* quote about divorce?' She raised a mischievous
eyebrow. 'Ah, yes. Zsa Zsa Gabor. "He taught me housekeeping; when I divorce I keep the house."'

He laughed. Delighted, relieved, intrigued—and *horny.*
'That explains how Willa got the house—who would dare
say no to *you*?'

'Lots of people dare—but there can only be one winner.
And I like the winner to be me.'

Scott's inner purr became a growl as his libido kicked
up a notch.

'Scott Knight—architect,' he said, holding out his hand.
'And expert inserter of foot into mouth.'

She took his hand in a firm, cool grip. Two mid-level
shakes—not wimpy, not crushing. Perfect.

'Nice to meet you, Scott Knight,' she said. 'And you're
more than welcome to roll out the lawyer jokes. Who knows?
There may even be one I haven't heard.'

'Ouch. Again. I'm going to need stitches.'

She retrieved her punch glass. 'Well, I have a needle and
thread.' Sipped. 'And a stapler too, if you prefer it a little…
rougher.'

His eyes skimmed her the way hers had him. She was
covered from neck to mid-thigh in snug black. Plain, plain,
plain—and off-the-chain sexy. Naked arms and legs. High

heels in nude. The little green handbag. Her red hair loose and gorgeous. And the lips—good God, the lips.

He felt a little shiver of excitement as he caught her scent. Tuberose. His favourite.

'You look like a tearer, not a repairer, to me,' he said, plucking the words more for their innuendo value than anything else. The only important thing was staying near her. He'd talk about knee replacements if that would keep her close.

'That's because I am,' she said. '"Ball-tearer" is the complete phrase, I believe.'

'You're not scaring me.'

'What *am* I doing?'

'You *know* what you're doing, Kate Cleary. You know very well. So let's cut to the chase. Are you hooked up with anyone? I mean, anyone I couldn't take out in a Rubik's cube tournament, obviously.' He held his breath, waiting for the answer. *No, no, no, please.*

'Is that your speciality? The Rubik's cube?'

'Well, I'm better with the cube than I am at hand-to-hand combat—although for you I could get a little gladiatorial. Certainly *with* you I could.'

'Then how fortunate that I am, indeed, single. So…do you need me to demonstrate my Rubik's cube abilities?'

'Exactly how limber are you with those nice, long, slim fingers?'

'Eleven seconds—limber enough.' The tip of her tongue came out, ran across her plump red top lip. 'But I can go slow.'

Scott's nostrils flared with the scent of her, the triumph of it. He edged closer, until they were almost but not quite touching. 'I'd like to see you go fast…*and* slow.'

She raised that eyebrow again. And, God, he knew—just from that—she would be awesome in bed. He was going to have to find out. Maybe tonight…

She tilted her head back. And there was a challenge in that. 'That's going to depend.'

'On…?'

'What you're offering.'

He was about to suggest they consider an early departure to negotiate the 'offer' when—*dammit*—Willa materialised, with Rob beside her. Okay, maybe she hadn't materialised—maybe she'd walked quite normally across the floor and he'd been too busy gagging with lust to notice. But, whatever, the interruption was so ill-timed he wanted to punch something.

'Kate, I'm so glad you've met Scott,' Willa said, all warm and thrilled and happy. 'He's not likely to be a client, though—he's the confirmed bachelor of Weeping Reef!'

Scott only just held back the wince. Because that made him sound either gay or like a player. Rob, at least, had the grace to wince *for* him and clap the hand of sympathy on his back.

Kate couldn't possibly think, even for a second, that he was gay. Not after the conversation they'd been having.

On the other hand… A player? Yeah, he admitted to that. But he liked to do his *own* warning off of women who had happily-ever-after in their sights—with charm and skill and softly negotiated ground rules that meant everyone had fun right up until the goodbye. He didn't need his friends making public service announcements to scare away prospective bedmates before he even got to the first kiss.

'Let's leave it at bachelor, shall we, Willa?' Scott suggested through slightly gritted teeth.

Willa, oblivious, turned to him. 'Oh, are you *not* a confirmed bachelor? I thought you said friends with benefits was as far as you ever intended to go? Not that there's anything wrong with that. At all. Of course.'

Scott stared at Willa, speechless. Rob blew out a *not laughing, I promise* breath. Kate was biting the inside of her cheek, in the same predicament as Rob.

'After what happened in the Whitsundays I—' At last Willa stopped. Blushed very prettily—as Willa did everything.

Scott was still staring, frozen, praying she was not going to finish that.

'Oh,' Willa said. 'Well. Anyway. Kate is the best family lawyer in Sydney, as well as being a wonderful, kind, compassionate—'

'Thank you, Willa,' Kate interrupted smoothly. 'But I'm not quite ready for sainthood.'

Scott, unfreezing, saw the flush of pink that slashed across Kate's high cheekbones—not pretty, *stunning*!—and decided it was time to take control of the conversation and get his seduction back on track.

Leaning into Willa conspiratorially, he said, 'I hear Kate's also a Rubik's cube champion.'

Kate choked on her punch, trying—again—not to laugh.

And somehow that made Scott want her even more. He needed to get her away from everyone immediately. Out onto the deck into that particular corner that he knew from previous forays at Willa's harbourside mansion was very private, screened by a giant pot plant.

But any chance of getting Kate alone was snatched from him by another of the old Weeping Reef gang, Amy, who landed in their midst—because Amy never merely *appeared* anywhere—accompanied by her flatmate Jessica, who'd become an honorary gang member despite never having been near the Whitsundays.

Seduction plans were officially on simmer—but not off the heat. Half an hour—that was all he needed. Half an hour and Kate Cleary would be his.

Amy gave Scott a smacking kiss on the cheek before enveloping Kate in a hug.

'Kate!' she squealed. 'It's been an age.'

Kate laughed as she returned the hug. 'Well, two weeks, anyway—you didn't drink so many mojitos at Fox that you've forgotten?'

What the hell...? Scott wondered if he was the only one of the group who'd never met Kate. Well—him and Willa's brother, Luke, who was still in Singapore. Was this some kind of Weeping Reef conspiracy? Would Chantal turn up at last—because God knew how he'd deal with that—and Brodie? He could picture Brodie sauntering over, snatching the heart of *another* of Scott's women…

Not that Kate was Scott's woman.

Jessica and Kate were hugging now. Okay—this was officially out of control. Even *Jessica* knew Kate?

'It wasn't the mojitos that were news at Fox,' Jessica said. 'It was one very particular martini.'

The blush was back on Kate's cheekbones. 'The less said about that the better,' she said with a theatrical shudder.

Scott was suddenly desperate to hear the story. 'You don't like martinis?' he asked—only to have Willa, Amy and Jessica burst out laughing.

He looked at Rob, who gave him a *don't ask me* shrug.

'It was a *dirty* martini,' Amy said, putting him out of his misery. 'Bought for her by Barnaby, my arch nemesis at work, who just happened to be drinking at Fox too. Blond, blue-eyed and gorgeous—that's Barnaby. Thinks he's God's gift to marketing. *And* to women. And to be honest, he kind of *is*. Just not to Kate.'

Kate shook her head, laughing, as though batting the subject away.

'It was the way he said "dirty",' Jessica put in, helping herself to a glass of punch. 'It's one thing being presented with a dirty martini. It's quite another to have it presented with a slimy pick-up line. *"Just how dirty do you like it, baby?"* Yep—that would make any woman want to jump you. *Not*.'

More laughing from the girls as Kate covered her eyes with a hand.

Rob was practically cringing. 'Seriously?'

Willa kissed Rob's cheek. 'Not all men are as evolved as you, Rob.'

Rob turned to Scott. 'You ever used that one?'

'Dirty martini? Nope. And, given the reaction Barnaby

got, I doubt I ever will. Although in my youth I did once embarrass myself with a comment to twin girls about a *Ménage à Trois*.'

Jessica's eyes bugged. 'Twins? Like…a real *ménage à trois*? Or is that the name of a fancy-pants cocktail?'

'It's a cocktail,' Scott assured her. 'And delicious, apparently—because, as it happens, they both ordered one and made very…*approving*…noises.' He cleared his throat, all faux embarrassment. 'As they sipped, I mean.'

'They ordered one apiece—with a side order of you?' Amy asked, batting her eyelashes outrageously.

Scott smiled. The lazy, teasing smile he reserved for flirty moments with women he wasn't ever going to take to bed. 'A gentleman never tells a lady's secrets.'

He saw something flash across Amy's face. Something like…distress? But it was gone so quickly he wondered if he'd imagined it. And the next moment she was laughing again.

'Well, anyway, enough with the "in my youth" talk. If I've got my arithmetic in order you're twenty-seven—one measly year older than me. And I'll have you know I still consider myself to be in my youth.'

An odd gasping sound from Kate had Scott turning to her. It looked as if she'd spilled punch on her dress, because she was brushing a hand over the bodice. It must have been only the tiniest drop—*he* certainly couldn't see any sign of it—but the next moment Willa was ushering Kate to the guest bathroom and Amy was asking Rob what exactly was in the punch, because she'd never seen Kate's nerves of steel so much as bend before, let alone be dented.

The punch, apparently, was a combination of vodka, white wine, white rum and champagne, with an occasional strawberry waved over the bowl—that did *not* sound girly! It was a miracle everyone in the house wasn't stumbling around breaking bits off sculptures, staggering into walls and pitching face-first into pot plants.

But Scott had a feeling the potency of the brew was not

the problem with Kate. She'd looked sort of *shocky*. Surely not because of that harmless *ménage à trois* talk? She was too sophisticated for that. It would take him two minutes, tops, to explain that away. Which would leave him twenty-eight minutes to charm her out of her panties.

But twenty minutes later Scott hadn't managed to get near Kate. Every time he took a step in her direction she moved somewhere else. As if she was on guard against him—which was crazy. Almost as crazy as what the sight of her loose-hipped, strolling, rolling walk was doing to his testosterone levels. Sexiest walk *ever*.

At the twenty-four-minute mark, as he made what felt like his hundredth attempt to reach her and she replaced the stroll with a dash—an actual freaking *dash*—towards a small group of people whose average age looked to be a hundred and four, he realised she really and truly *was* on her guard.

Oh, my God.

He was chasing her and she was running away. This had never, ever happened to him before.

And as he watched her, trying to figure out what the hell had gone wrong, the last six minutes of his self-allocated thirty minutes' seduction time ticked away…and she was gone.

Disappeared. Like Cinderella, but wearing both of her take-me-now shoes.

He fingered the card she'd given him.

Weird. Very, *very* weird. A mystery. What had he said? Done?

Well, Scott loved mysteries. And challenges. And women who wore red lipstick.

And he was suddenly very certain that this thing between him and Kate Cleary—because there was definitely a thing—was not going to end with a drop of spilled punch and no explanation.

He looked at her card again, noted the address—a block from his city office.

Easy.

CHAPTER TWO

KATE LET HERSELF into her apartment, tossed her bag onto the couch, kicked off her shoes, wiggled her toes…and let out a tortured groan that had nothing to do with her sore feet and everything to do with the divorce party.

Which had been a disaster.

She couldn't believe she'd been smut-talking about a stapler and a Rubik's cube. As bad as Dirty Martini Barnaby! Flirting with that hot, gorgeous hunk like a horny teenager.

And then to discover that the hot, gorgeous hunk practically *was* a horny teenager…

She let out another tortured groan.

Not that twenty-seven really *was* teenaged.

But she was thirty-two, for God's sake! A *my way or the highway* woman of thirty-two!

She opened the French doors and stepped onto the expansive terrace of her apartment. She'd chosen the apartment for the view—not the Harbour Bridge in the distance, even though that was her favourite Sydney landmark, but the boats. Something about them, bobbing gently in Rushcutters Bay, soothed her. The escape daydream, she called it. Sailing away from her troubles to a world of possibilities. A world of adventure…

She tried to bring herself back to earth by reminding herself of the time she'd forced the husband of one of her clients to sell his boat and hand over half the cash and he'd cried like a baby. But even the memory of that less than edifying spectacle couldn't stop her thinking about adventures and possibilities.

And tonight, very specifically, the possibility of an adventure with Scott Knight.

The image of him was so clear in her head. That killer body—tall, broad, strong. The slightly spiky mid-brown hair. The alertness of his cool, pale green eyes. That *I've got a secret* smile that was kind of calculating…and somehow intriguing exactly because of that. She'd wanted to twist him into a sexual pretzel the moment she'd heard his lazy, drawling voice—a voice so at odds with the alert intelligence in his eyes it was almost a challenge.

But…*twenty-seven years old*?

She covered her face with her hands and let fly with one more tortured groan.

Pent-up need—that was the problem. It had been a long time between…cocktails. Dirty Martini, Bosom Caresser, Between the Sheets, Sex on the Beach or any other kind. A *damned* long time.

Well, she clearly couldn't be trusted to see Scott Knight again until that pent-up need had been met. She would have to make sure any Weeping Reef gathering was Scott-free before attending. In fact, she'd go one step further and stick to girls-only catch-ups when it came to Willa. So just Willa, Amy, Jessica and the other girl she had yet to meet—Chantal—if she ever showed. No Rob. No Scott. Luke was in Singapore, and the other guy whose name started with a B—Brady? No, Brodie—hadn't turned up at anything yet. So the whole girls-only thing was definitely doable.

And in the meantime she would find some other man to twist into a sexual pretzel. Someone like Phillip, a barrister who was happily divorced, suave, cultured and—at forty years old—mature. In the right age ballpark.

Then she would let the girls know she was taken, word would find its way to Scott, and that would be that.

Yes, Phillip would do very nicely. She would give him a call on Monday and arrange to catch up with him at the bar near her office for a Slow Comfortable Screw. A Strawberry Stripper. A Sex Machine. Or…or *something*.

* * *

Monday morning for Kate began with an eight o'clock client meeting.

Kate always felt like cuddling this particular client. Fragile, timid Rosie, who crept into her office as though she'd like
a corner to hide in. Rosie was so intimidated by her husband
she couldn't even bring herself to tell him he was making
her unhappy—so how she was going to raise the subject of
divorce was anyone's guess.

It was not a position a *Cleary* woman would ever find
herself in!

Her frustrating meeting with Rosie reminded Kate how
happy she was not to be married. And that, in turn, prompted
her to get to the task of calling the equally gamophobic Phillip to arrange that bar meeting. A highly satisfactory phone
call that took four businesslike minutes.

Two meetings later she made herself a cup of coffee and
opened her diary to recheck her schedule…and blinked.

Blinked, blinked, blinked.

She called her no-nonsense, indeterminately aged, absolutely superb assistant. 'What's this appointment at twelve-
thirty today, Deb?'

'Hang on…' Keyboard clicks. 'Oh, Scott Knight. He called
while you were with your eight o'clock. Said he'd mentioned
a lunch appointment when he saw you on Saturday night.'

Kate slumped back in her chair, awed—and depressingly
delighted—at the presumption of it.

'Oh, did he?' she asked, trying to sound ominous.

'So he *didn't*?' Chuckle. 'Well, I did wonder why you
hadn't mentioned it to me, but he sounded… Well, let's keep
it clean and say *nice*, so I made an executive decision and
slotted him in.'

'Yes, he does sound "nice",' Kate said dryly, and smiled
at Deb's sudden crack of laughter.

'Want me to cancel him, hon? Leave you to your takeaway
chicken and mung-bloody-bean salad?'

Kate opened her mouth to say an automatic yes—but into her head popped an image of Rosie that morning. Diffident. Nervous. Panicky. Dodging her husband rather than telling him their marriage was over.

And hot on the heels of that came the memory of her own behaviour on Saturday night, dodging Scott at Willa's party. So unnerved by the force of her attraction to him she'd mapped out an actual plan for seeing only Willa, Amy and Jessica. *Crazy.* She should be able to see her friends whenever and wherever she wanted, without giving a second thought to whoever else might just happen to be in the vicinity.

As if she couldn't handle a *twenty-seven-year-old*!

And on her own turf…in her own office? Easy.

This would not be like the divorce party, where the kick of lust had taken her by surprise. She would be prepared for it today. And she could tell him directly, herself, that she was no longer in the market—so thanks, but no thanks.

'Kate?' Deb prompted. 'Shall I cancel him?'

Kate straightened her shoulders. 'No, that's fine,' she said. 'It will take approximately five minutes to conclude my business with Mr Knight. Plenty of time to eat chicken and mung-bloody-bean salad afterwards.' She nodded, satisfied. 'Now, can you grab me the McMahon file? There's something I need to check before the parties arrive to have another crack at a settlement conference.'

'Mmm-hmm. Settlement conference… That's what they're calling World War III these days, is it?'

Scott, no stranger to wooing women, brought flowers to Kate's office. Nothing over the top. Just simple, colourful gerberas that said *I'm charming so I don't have to bring roses.*

Not that he saw any softening in Deb's face as he handed over the bunch.

'Seems a shame to spend money on flowers when you're only going to be in there for five minutes,' she said.

'Oh, they're not for Kate,' Scott said. 'They're for you.'

'Even so…' Deb said, but he didn't miss the tiny sparkle that sprang to life in her eyes. 'Her meeting is running over time. Take a seat, if you'd like to wait.'

Scott angled himself so he could see through the glass wall of the boardroom. Could see *her*. Kate.

She was sitting at a long table, her back to him. Beside her was an overly blonded, expensive-looking woman wearing lime-green. The client, obviously. On the opposite side of the table was a man who epitomised lawyerdom. Pinstriped suit, white shirt, conservative tie. Beside Pinstripe was a man who looked as if he'd spent too long on the tanning bed, wearing an open-necked shirt with a humungous gold chain visible against his chest. Gold Chain was holding a dog. A furry little dog. Which he kept petting.

Amongst the four of them—five, if you included the dog— there were frequent vehement headshakes, very occasional nods, hand gestures aplenty. At one point Kate ran a hand tiredly over her hair, which was tied in a low ponytail. It made Scott want to touch her.

And that reminded him that their only physical contact on Saturday night had been a handshake. So it was kind of nuts to be so obsessed with her. But obsessed was what he was.

Suddenly Kate stood. She put her hands on the table and leaned forward—making a particular point, he guessed. She was wearing a cream skirt suit. Beautifully, tightly fitted.

Scott was appreciating the view of her really superb back-side when she stretched just a little bit further forward and her skirt hitched up for one split second. Just long enough to give him a tiny glimpse of the lacy band at the top of one of her…*ooohhh*…*stockings*.

She was wearing *stockings*.

All the blood in Scott's body redirected itself in one gush, straight to his groin. The sudden ache of it made him clamp his jaws together.

Stockings!

Stay-ups? Suspenders? Hell, who cared which?

Then she was back in her seat. Scott realised he'd been holding his breath and exhaled—very, very slowly.

He forced his eyes away from her—scared he'd start drooling otherwise—and saw Gold Chain give the dog a kiss on the nose while keeping his eyes on his wife across the table.

That seemed to incense Blondie—which Scott could understand, because it *was* kind of gross—who leapt to her feet and screeched so loudly her voice bounced straight through the glass wall. Next moment all four of them were standing. There were waved arms, pointed fingers, even a stamped foot. The stamped foot was from Blondie, who was then subtly restrained by Kate, who seemed serene in the midst of chaos. Pinstripe was using a similar restraining movement on Gold Chain, but was somewhat hampered by the dog snapping at him.

Scott heard a few words shouted—hurled. *Custody. Holidays. Missed drop-offs.* Interspersed with an occasional ear-sizzling foul-mouthed curse.

Shocked, Scott looked at Deb. Shouldn't she be calling the cops before someone threw an actual punch? But Deb just kept typing, unperturbed. Which would have to mean that Kate put up with such crap routinely, wouldn't it? Did that explain Kate's air of cynicism at Willa's divorce party? Because if this was divorce, it sure wasn't pretty.

He tuned back in to the screeches. A custody battle? Had to be. The antagonists were…what?…in their early thirties, maybe? So the kids had to be young. How *many* kids?

Scott wondered how his own parents would have handled a custody battle. Not that his parents would have done anything so undignified as get divorced. The joining of two old families, the merging of two fortunes, had been destiny working the way it was supposed to—even if he'd never seen his parents kiss, let alone hold hands. Their merger was too perfect ever to be classified as a mistake, so that sucker wasn't getting dissolved.

But if they *had* divorced he couldn't imagine them getting into a raging custody battle. Over *him*, at any rate. They would have come up with a simple, bloodless schedule of visits, complete with taxi pick-ups and drop-offs.

Custody of his older brother would have been a different story. There would have been nothing amicable about sharing the 'perfect' son. Maybe that was the real reason they'd stayed together—the inability to satisfactorily halve his brother.

And what an opportune moment for the boardroom door to be opening, so he could stop thinking.

Gold Chain was coming out, carrying the dog, speaking furiously to his solicitor. Pinstripe had a grip on his client's dog-free arm and was dealing admirably with dodging the growling dog's snapping jaws as he walked Gold Chain past Deb's desk and out of the suite. Kate and her client stayed in the room talking for a few minutes, but then they too appeared. Kate was nodding, her red-lipsticked mouth pursed in sympathy.

Kate caught sight of him—and slashes of pink zapped along her cheekbones as if by Magic Marker. And then she returned her concentration to Blondie.

'It's not good enough,' Blondie was saying. 'He keeps returning her late. If it doesn't stop I'll be rethinking the money. Make sure he knows that, Kate.'

A few soothing words, an unrelenting shepherding towards the suite exit. Out through the door.

And then…silence.

Deb looked at Scott. Raised her eyebrows. That little sparkle was in her eyes again.

Scott raised his eyebrows back, a little shell-shocked and a lot awed at what Kate had just put up with. And still somewhat gobsmacked that such a small dog could be so nasty. He'd back that dog against a pitbull.

And then Kate was coming back. Smiling coolly—very lawyer-like and professional.

'Scott,' she said, and held out her hand.

Scott shook it. 'Kate,' he said, and could hear the laughter in his voice. Less than forty-eight hours ago they'd been heading for sex. Today he got a handshake.

No. Just…*no*.

Kate gestured to the office next to the boardroom. Scott walked ahead of her, opened the heavy wooden door and stood just inside, taking in the dignified space. Carpeted floor. Big desk. Behind the desk a large tinted window on the outside world. Large window on the inside world too—untinted—through which he could see Kate speaking to Deb, because the Venetian blinds that were there for privacy were open. Neat, modern filing cabinets. Two black leather chairs in front of her desk. Vivid knock-out painting on one wall—the only splash of colour.

And then Kate was entering, closing the door behind her. He turned to face her. She was close. So close. Cream suit. Red hair. Those other-worldly grey eyes. Tuberose scent.

Just for a second the memory of the top of her stocking burst in his head.

And drove him wild.

Which had to be why he grabbed her by the upper arms, backed her up a step, pushed her against that nice solid door and covered her mouth with his.

CHAPTER THREE

FOR ONE FRANTIC SECOND he felt Kate stiffen.

God, don't stop me. I'll die if you stop me.

He licked her mouth—her gorgeous, red, luscious mouth—and with an inarticulate sound that was half-moan, half-whimper she opened to him.

Thank you, thank you, thank you.

His tongue swooped inside, tangled with hers...and she was everything he'd hoped she would be. Delicious, and hot, and desperate—as desperate as he was. She tasted so good. Smelled like heaven. Felt lush and ripe against him as he pressed her to the door. He wished he could get her closer—although that was knuckleheaded. If he pushed any harder against her they'd be through the wood, spilling onto the floor at the base of Deb's desk. And exhibitionism wasn't high on his must-do list.

Then Kate's arms circled him and he *was* closer. *Miracle.* She tore the shirt loose from his pants and then her hands were under the cotton, sliding up his back, down, then up. Rushing over his skin. No finesse, just raw, hungry possession. Restless, seeking, sweeping...

He heard her whimper, low in her throat, and it set off a flare in his head. He wanted every part of her in his hands all at once. Impossible lust. Outrageous. He grabbed the back of her head, bringing their mouths together so furiously their teeth clashed. But he didn't stop and neither did she. They were straining together. He could feel her heart thudding against his own rocketing beats. He wished he could see her naked. Needed to touch her bare skin.

Alone. He needed them to be alone.

Keeping his burning mouth fused to Kate's, he reached,

one-handed, grabbing for the cord that controlled the Venetian blinds. He scrabbled there, cursing inside his impatient head until he found it, yanked. *Close, dammit, close!* And then the blinds came clattering down and they were invisible—just him and Kate, wrapped together—and he was going to take her in some way, by God!

Next second they were spinning, fast and clumsy, and with one rough push it was *his* back jammed against the door, and he was sucking in gasping breaths with every tiny *get it while you can* break in their hungry kisses. Her hands were under his shirt again almost before the thud against the wood sounded his willing submission. Skating, racing up to his shoulders, over his chest, across his sides, down his stomach. Then she was reaching for his belt, undoing, unbuttoning, unzipping, her hands diving to touch, to grip him through his underwear.

He cradled her head, hands digging in to keep her mouth fused to his. Felt her hair—cool silk against his fingers. He must have wrenched the band from it because it was loose. They were almost at eye level—and that reminded him she was wearing high heels. The thought of those heels, her legs, made him groan. The memory of the top of her stocking— that one hot glimpse—was ferocious in his head. He wanted to see those stockings, wanted her legs wrapped around him.

His hands moved to her perfect backside. Tight and sexy and…*covered*. Not good enough. Not now. His hands went lower, down to her thighs. He stopped for a blinding moment as her hand squeezed him and he thought he'd lose it, but determinedly he moved on. The stockings. He had to feel them…touch them.

The instant his fingers reached the hem of her skirt he yanked it up. Out of the way. Out of *his* way. *God, God, God,* he'd reached that lacy edge. He could feel the band, snug against her slender thigh. *Oooohhhhh. G-o-o-o-d.* So damned *hot*. Fingers toyed at the edge for long moments, tracing the skin at the very top, then sliding up, over her bottom, now covered only by soft, slippery silk. He groaned into her mouth. He had to have her—*now*.

She spread her legs to accommodate his straining erection between her thighs, pulled him hard into the cradle of her, wordless and panting.

'I want to see you,' he said.

But before she could respond he was backing her further into the room. Step, kiss…step, kiss…step, kiss. And then they were at her desk, her thighs hitting the desktop. Her amazing, stockinged thighs. Just the thought of them had his fingers twitching to touch.

'Open your legs,' he said, and she did.

And then his fingers were there, feeling the damp silk. He was too desperate to be gentle, wrenching the covering aside so his fingers could dip into her. Urgently slipping inside her, then out, circling, then in, out, circling again. She cried out and he plastered his mouth to hers, bending her backwards at the same time as his arm swooped, scattering everything off the desk onto the floor.

He heard the thump and clatter—didn't care. Her back was on the desk, her bottom at the edge, her legs splayed and dangling, her feet in their sexy high heels just touching the floor. He was between her thighs, fingers still working, resolutely wringing wordless cries from her. He hadn't stopped kissing her, scared to break that mouth-to-mouth bond in case she told him to stop. He couldn't stop now—didn't want to stop.

Fingers still moving against her, he used his other hand to wrench her skirt higher until he knew—even though he couldn't yet see—that she was exposed to him.

He imagined the picture: pale fabric bunched around her hips, silky knickers covering her except for the slight skew at her core where his fingers played, the stay-up stockings in an understated nude that just made them that much sexier. *Steam*. He thought he must have steam coming out of his ears. Hell, he wanted to see that picture.

Okay—he would have to risk freeing her mouth just so he *could* see that picture.

He pulled back and Kate reached automatically to push her skirt down, but his hands stayed hers.

'No. I have to see. I *have* to, Kate.'

Throwing her head back, she let her hands drop to her sides, open to him.

He pulled back, looked long and hard, while his heart threatened to leap out through his eyeballs and he thought he might actually come on the spot. Violet. A flash of purple amongst the cream and nude. That delicious part of her just peeping out at the side. She was the most gloriously sexy thing he had ever seen in his life. He had a feeling the image of Kate Cleary on the desk, spread for him, would be the hottest memory of his life.

He made some low, growling noise—like an animal, because he *felt* like an animal—and knew he had to get at her the fastest way he could. No condom—because why would he need a condom just to see her briefly in her office on a Monday afternoon? *Idiot—don't leave home without one ever again.* So it would be his fingers and his mouth.

Even before the thought had finished he was on her, his fingers there, renewing their endless dipping slide. He dropped to his knees, watching each undulating movement of her hips. And when that wasn't enough he tugged that violet silk a little further off centre and put his mouth on her.

She bucked, cried out, as his tongue replaced his fingers, as his hands moved to grasp her hips and bring her closer to his mouth, angling her so he could explore every delicious fold and crease. The taste of her was intoxicating. The scent of her arousal, the feel of her as he suckled the pearly clitoris he'd freed from the silk…

'Delicious,' he said, between long, slow pulls. 'I knew you would be.'

And then she was whimpering in earnest, soft mewing cries as he alternated the pressure, building the fire in her with every scrap of skill and care he had, building, building… One last, long, endless, sucking kiss there and her hips bucked off the desk.

And then a low, throaty moan was torn out of her as she came and her hands fisted convulsively in his hair, dragging him into her moist heat, and he was breathing her in as he laved her with his eager, lusting tongue, so damned *hot* for her.

He stayed there, his mouth on her, until the waves receded.

And then her legs relaxed and she lay like an exhausted doll, legs spread, limp hands slipping from his hair as he stood back and looked at her. She was so wantonly beautiful to Scott's still hungry eyes that he had to cover his face with his hands—because he wanted to be inside her so badly the sight of her was painful.

A heartbeat later he heard the soft sounds of her getting herself together—sitting up, adjusting her clothes. He dropped his hands a millimetre at a time, gauging his control as he went.

Okay.

She was covered.

He could breathe.

Sort of.

That spectacular blush was on her cheekbones. 'What about…about you?' she asked. 'I mean…you. You know…'

Scott winced. 'That's what I get for not packing a condom,' he said, and pulled up his gaping pants, refastening the openings Kate had wrenched apart earlier. He tucked in his shirt. 'Not that I expected… Well, not that I expected *that.*'

Her eyes darted to the Venetian blinds as she edged off the desk and he read her relief as she puffed out a little breath. Had she not even noticed that he'd closed the blinds? That said something about the passion between them.

'So, Kate, I'd say you owe me,' he said. 'And I have an inkling you're not the kind of woman who likes to be in anyone's debt, so I'll collect tonight. Name the place. Name the time.'

She bent to pick up the various objects Scott had so unceremoniously shoved off the desk. Including her laptop, which she didn't even bother checking for damage.

Ordinarily he would have helped. But not now. Now he just watched. She was doing something inside her head. Calculating. Planning. So best to be a spectator, gathering clues from her demeanour. What was she thinking?

She picked up a box of tissues, but instead of putting it back on the desk she held it out to him. 'Lipstick,' she said, gesturing to his mouth.

He plucked a tissue from the box. '*Still* there?' he asked, giving her his most wicked smile. 'After my mouth was so busy between your—'

'Yes, still there,' she cut in.

Her voice was curt, no-nonsense...but he saw the shiver tremble through her body as she put the tissue box back in its place on her desk.

And then she checked her watch. Followed that with a stride over to the Venetians to open them with one sharp tug of the cord.

'Oh, no, Katie,' Scott said at that point. 'We don't get back to normal and move on to our next appointments after *that*.'

She looked at him. 'Kate. Not Katie.' She licked her top lip. Again. Eyes closed. Then opened. And then she threw her hands out with a *you win* sigh. 'All right—fair enough. Let's talk.'

She waved him to one of the black leather chairs as she walked around behind the desk and settled into her own intimidating, high-backed number.

'That was a mistake,' she said, very direct.

'I made one mistake—I didn't bring a condom. Otherwise that went pretty much as I would have liked.'

'I don't do relationships,' Kate said, ignoring that.

'Really?'

'Really.'

'Perfect.'

'What does that mean?'

'You don't do relationships. I don't do relationships. But I *do* do sex…and so, obviously, do you. And very well too.'

She stared at him for a long moment. Then that little lick of the top lip again—God, he wanted to be the one licking it.

'I have someone,' she said.

That brought a frown—fast and hard and very displeased. 'You told me at the party you didn't.'

'I'm seeing him tonight. We're working out an arrangement.'

'What kind of arrangement?'

She looked at him out of those clear eyes. 'A mutually satisfactory "friends with benefits" arrangement.'

'Work out an arrangement with me instead.'

'Phillip is forty.'

'Past his sexual prime.'

'Closer to my age.'

'How old are you, Katie?'

'Thirty-two. And it's Kate.'

'Then he's not closer to your age—I am. Five years versus eight years. And I want you more.'

'How could you possibly know that?'

'Because nobody could want you more than I do.' He leaned forward in his chair. 'And you owe me. One orgasm.'

'I'm not interested in having a toy boy.'

'And I'm not interested in being one.' He stared at her, wondering… And then he relaxed back in his chair. 'Aha! So *that* was it.'

'What are you talking about?'

'What happened at the party to make you run away. Amy said I was twenty-seven.'

'I don't do relationships.'

'Yeah—we covered that one.'

'People who are twenty-seven are in the prime age bracket for relationships.'

'Newsflash—so are people who are thirty-two.'

'I'm not like other thirty-two-year-olds.'

'And I'm not like other twenty-seven-year-olds. Remember? I'm the confirmed bachelor of Weeping Reef.'

'You said bachelor, but not *confirmed*.'

'I lied because I didn't want to scare you off.'

'Not exactly honourable.'

'That's because I'm not honourable. I have not one honourable intention when I look at you. Which won't bother you since you're not interested in relationships. So, Katie, you're going to have to tell your forty-year-old he's too late. Unless you didn't like what just happened…?'

Kate leaned back in her chair. Licked her top lip again, which was now almost bare of lipstick. It was heavy, brooding. He wanted it on his body.

'There's no reason I won't like it with Phillip just as much,' she said.

'What—you'd let Phillip go down on you on your desk during business hours, would you?'

'He wouldn't want to.'

'And that's why I'm the man for you. Because I would. I *did*. And I would do it again in a heartbeat, Katie.'

'Kate. And it's not a matter of liking. It's a matter of being clear what the end-game is so nobody gets hurt.'

'I don't get hurt.'

She looked startled. 'Everyone gets hurt.'

'Not me.'

'You've never been hurt?'

Scott's body tensed. *Redirect.* 'Let me put it this way. There's no need for either of us to get hurt. You mentioned the end-game. Why can't the end-game be sex? Pure and simple sex?'

Kate had picked up a pen and was tap, tap, tapping it on the desk. 'Pure and simple sex,' she said slowly. 'No strings?'

'You got it.'

Long moment. Tap, tap, tap. 'And if I were to lay some ground rules…? You wouldn't have a problem with that?'

'Lay away.'

'I'd need time. To think it through. Come up with an agreement.'

'I'm sure you already have the ground rules worked out for old man Phillip.'

'He's not old.'

'So your age fixation only works one way?'

No answer.

Scott smiled the Number One smile—*I am available for sex immediately*—as he got out his business card and tossed it onto her desk. 'You've got until I see you tonight to work out whatever rules you want—but, just to be clear, whether we come to an agreement or not, you owe me. If I leave this office and you suddenly have second thoughts about embarking on an affair with me, you still owe me. You. Owe. Me. And I'm not leaving until you give me a time and a place for tonight where you're going to pay me back. Katie. So let's have it.'

She was thinking—he could almost see her brain fizzing.

And then, 'Seven o'clock,' she announced. 'Come to my apartment.' She scribbled something on a sheet of paper and held it out to him. 'That's the address. And it's Kate.'

Scott reached for the paper, pocketed it.

Kate stood, walked around the desk to the door, opened it.

Scott got to his feet more slowly and followed her. But something about the controlled expression on her face got to him—so instead of walking out and heading merrily on his way, he stopped beside her, grabbed her upper arms, tugged her close and slammed his mouth hard on hers. Long, hot moment. Framed in the doorway for anyone who happened to be in the suite to see.

He released her just as suddenly, and smiled to see the combination of shock and desire on her face as he drew back.

'You've got no idea how much I'm going to need that debt paid when I see you at seven tonight,' he said softly.

And with that, he turned to wink at the unabashedly staring Deb and sauntered towards the exit.

As he reached it he heard Deb's voice. 'That was some five minutes, Kate. So, what will it be? Chicken and mung beans? Or do you need something more substantial—a chunk of raw meat, perhaps—to get your strength back?'

CHAPTER FOUR

RACING HOME AFTER WORK that evening, Kate was kicking herself for not going with her first instinct and simply supplanting Phillip with Scott at the bar. A quick twist of an arrangement already in place. Same bar. Same purpose. Just a different model.

She didn't know why the invitation to her apartment had popped out of her mouth instead.

Although, thinking back to that hot scene on her desk—God, her *desk*!—she figured it was probably just as well she'd gone for a more private option. If she couldn't control herself with Scott in her place of work, with Deb sitting just outside the door, how could she trust herself not to perform her payback sex act in the bar, on her knees under the table?

An image that got her so turned on she switched the water temperature of the shower to cold before getting under the spray.

Lust was still fizzing under her skin when she got out, so choosing something to wear took on a whole new meaning—because it had to be something that could come off easily.

Forgoing underwear, she grabbed a loose, tissue-thin shift in a rich russet colour. *Very* easy to take off when the moment came. And she hoped the outline of her body under the fine silk would drive Scott a little crazy in the meantime—payback for how crazy he'd driven *her*.

She left her hair loose. Put on a minimum of make-up. No lipstick—her mouth was going to be all over him, and she didn't want to leave a trail over his clothes or his skin.

She was so full of nervous energy, she caught herself pacing the floor while she waited for him. At this rate one touch of his clever fingers would have her unravelling—and she was *not* going to unravel twice in one day! She poured herself a glass of very cold white wine and forced her fidgety limbs onto the couch, trying to summon at least a semblance of composure.

The intercom buzzed at six fifty-nine p.m. and she closed her eyes, taking a deep breath. *This was it.*

As she let Scott in she ran her eyes over his body—white T-shirt, jeans. Very cool, very gorgeous. Her eyes kept going. Down to his...

Oh.

Converse All Star sneakers.

Cool, gorgeous...and *young.*

Those sneakers were *not* something forty-year-old Phillip would wear.

Twenty-seven. Okay, wake-up call. What the hell had she been thinking? She forced her eyes away from his feet, up to his eyes, preparing to tell him the deal was off.

But the look on his face gave her pause.

Kate had never seen such taut grimness—and she'd seen some very grim faces in the courtroom. His look got more taut and even more grim as he ran his eyes over her dress, all the way down to her bare feet and back up.

'Is something wrong?' she asked, alarmed.

'Yes,' he said, and his voice was every bit as grim as his face. 'I've been replaying that scene in your office in my head all afternoon, and I'm so desperate to get my hands on you I can't think straight. So let's skip the pleasantries.'

He nodded at the glass of wine on the coffee table.

'I don't want the drink you're probably going to offer me. I'm not into mood music, so don't bother asking me what I want to listen to. No need for a tour of the apartment—I can see it's nice and modern and open-plan. Don't give a rat's about the view. And the only thing I want to eat is you. *Again.*' Strained smile. 'Now, are we doing the ground rules before or after I get my orgasm?'

'Before,' Kate said, any thought of backing away from

their agreement obliterated by the heat of his words, the wild rush of desire that bolted through her.

'Then let's do it fast. Before I explode.'

The air was thick with lust as she guided him to the dining table, handed him the pages she'd prepared for their signatures.

'So we're—what?' he asked. 'Signing a contract?'

She nodded. 'With a contract we'll both know where we stand, what we can expect. It keeps things uncomplicated.'

Scott laughed, but didn't refuse, so Kate started running through the clauses.

She didn't even make it through the first one before Scott cut her off. 'Katie—you want a contract, then a contract it is. But it's a sex contract—not a pre-nup or a business merger. And it's not even legally enforceable, as we both know. So can you just give me the basics? Then I'll sign—there's no way I won't—and we can move on to implementing it. Because if I have to see your nipples poking against that dress for much longer without touching you, I am going to go freaking insane.'

The sudden throb between Kate's thighs had her squirming on her chair.

'I see I'm not the only one eager to get to the implementation stage,' he said, and with an inarticulate *I give up* growl reached out to cup one of her breasts through the silk.

She felt her nipple tighten even further. He pinched it gently, once. She gasped, he groaned, and then he wrenched his hand away and shot out of his seat.

'Going to need a drink after all,' he said. 'No—don't get up. Faster if I get it myself while you start going through the rules.' He headed for her kitchen, with a final prompt. 'Come on, Katie. Get it done for pity's sake. I can hear you, I can see you—go.'

'Right,' she said. *Basics.* Basics were good. Fast was good. The sooner they agreed on the terms, the sooner she could have him.

Cupboard opening…clacking of a glass on the kitchen counter.

'Two nights per week,' she said.

Fridge door opening…closing. 'What if I want more?'

'Two per week is the minimum. We can negotiate additional days as required.'

He was pouring. 'Okay. Next.'

'Any costs incurred in pursuit of mutual sexual pleasure to be split fifty-fifty.'

He was back with his wine. 'I can live with that.'

'No public displays of affection.'

He was sitting. 'Done,' he said. 'Nauseating stuff, PDAs.'

'No kissing unless it's sex-related.'

Scott held up a 'stop' hand. 'Hang on. When is kissing between an unrelated man and woman ever *not* sex-related?'

She was blushing—she could feel it. Because this was an embarrassing clause. It presupposed he would *want* to kiss her outside of sex. But kisses led to affection. And trouble lay down that road. So, embarrassing or not, it was best to have it covered in advance.

'I mean no kisses hello, goodbye—that sort of thing,' she said. 'Only kisses that lead to or are the result of sex.'

Scott looked at her mouth for a long moment. She thought he was going to object. But then he shrugged.

'Okay,' he said. 'Go on.'

'Fantasies,' Kate said, and felt the blush deepen.

'We get *fantasies*?' Scott asked reverently. 'Yee-ha!'

Kate rolled her eyes, but she was smiling. 'I thought you'd like that part of the deal. There are still rules, however. I'm suggesting a start phrase—if one or the other of us decides to enact a fantasy, a text message with "Play Time" is all that's required—along with the date, time and place. And, of course, any outfits, devices and accessories will be provided by the fantasy's owner.'

'If you could see inside my mind…'

Kate laughed. 'I'm sure I'll be seeing what's inside it very soon. But in addition to a start phrase we'll need a trigger word which, when said, will stop the activity should one of us become uncomfortable with what's happening.'

'Why not just "stop"?'

'Because that might be part of the fantasy—either a version of "stop" or "don't stop". Or it could mean "pause" or "wait" just as easily as it could mean "no more". Better to have something unambiguous. Like…maybe…a name? Something that couldn't be mistaken for anything else and wouldn't have anything to do with sex.'

Scott smiled—a particularly cool smile that made his eyes look like ice. 'Let's go with "Hugo", in that case,' he said.

'Hugo?'

'I can assure you that will stop me in my tracks.'

'Fine,' Kate agreed. 'I don't know any Hugos, so it won't be confusing for me.'

'What else?' Scott asked, hands clenching and unclenching with impatience.

'We're up to confidentiality. The details of this contract must remain confidential.'

'Okay. Are we done?'

'Last point. Fidelity is assumed—'

'Absolutely,' Scott agreed promptly. 'I don't share.'

'I haven't finished. Fidelity is assumed, but should an unforeseen sexual encounter occur with someone other than the two parties covered by the agreement—if you or I—'

'Yes,' he interrupted. 'I know what you mean. If you sleep with someone other than me; if I do someone other than you…'

'Yes. If that happens it must be confessed prior to the resumption of any contracted sexual activity between us.'

But it seemed Scott had reached his limit.

He whipped the pages out of Kate's hand, grabbed the pen, flipped to the final clause, scratched out some words, added something and initialled the changes.

'That's my input,' he said. 'No infidelity or the contract is null and void.'

Kate thought about insisting that it remain, because fidelity was for real relationships and this was not one of those—but in all honesty it was a relief. She'd seen too much of the aftermath of infidelity to be sanguine about it under any circumstances.

So... 'All right,' she said. 'Should one of us seek our pleasure elsewhere, the agreement is broken.'

'You won't need to look elsewhere, Katie. I'll keep you so busy you'll be begging for a break.'

He picked up the pen again, ready to sign.

'Wait,' Kate said, snatching the pen from him before he could put it to paper. She licked nervously at her top lip. 'Scott, I think you should read the contract properly before you sign. You've found one clause you didn't like—there may be some wording that's unclear, or something else you're uncomfortable with when you have time to think about it. And I don't want to feel like I'm taking advantage of your youth.'

Scott's eyes narrowed. 'I'm twenty-seven—not stupid,' he said. 'And I hope we're not going to waste a lot of time talking about my age. Otherwise I'll be calling "Play Time" pretty damned fast and spanking you—and that's not even a fantasy of mine.'

'Not? Really?'

'Really. Not into pain—giving or receiving.'

'No spanking. Got it. Good. But, back on topic, you're not as experienced with the law as I am, so—'

'Boring subject. And not *germane*—there's a lawyer word for you, to prove that not all twenty-seven-year-olds are ignorant morons. I just love lawyer words.'

'Yes, but—'

'Am I deeding my firstborn child to you?'

'No.'

'Am I beholden to you for the rest of my life?'

'No—just a month. Through to the twenty-eighth of February.'

'Maybe I'd better read the contract, then, because that's not going to work for us unless there's an automatic rollover in there. Considering the size and intensity of my hard-on all three times I've been near you, I'm going to need longer than a month to do you every way I want to.'

Kate took a long, slow, silent breath. She'd never been with a man who talked so blatantly about sex. It should have been a turn-off—so why did it have the opposite effect? She had the feeling that if Scott Knight had bought her a martini and asked *'Just how dirty do you like it?'* she would have offered to show him on the spot.

'Yes,' she said, 'there is a rollover option in there.'

'Right—so give me the damned pen.'

Kate watched as he scrawled his signature.

It made a funny feeling erupt in her stomach—almost as if she owned a part of him with that one dashed name. For a moment it frightened her. She didn't want to own him. Didn't want him to own *her*. Not in any way, shape or form.

He handed her the pen and she hesitated.

'They're your rules,' Scott said, reading her easily. 'So sign.'

She signed.

And then Scott pushed his chair back from the table, looked across at her. All that grimness was back, tenfold.

'Now, come here,' he said.

CHAPTER FIVE

KATE WALKED OVER to him.

'I love that dress,' he said. '*Love* that dress. But take it off.'

Kate forced herself to go slowly as she reached for the sides of the dress and started to roll the fine silk between her fingertips, raising the hem gradually. Their first experience, in the office, had been frantic and fast, sudden and shocking and blind. This time she wanted to control it. To offer herself to him one piece at a time. Tease him. Wow him.

Payback.

Scott leaned forward in his seat, eyes intent on the hem inching upwards, until she reached her upper thighs. She paused there as Scott's breathing became harsher, choppier. One more roll. Another. Bringing the hem higher up, up—until she was exposed from the hips down.

She saw Scott swallow as his eyes focused. 'Like fire…' he whispered. 'Come closer.'

Kate took two steps until she was standing an arm's length away. He reached out to touch, smoothed his fingers over the narrow strip of dark red hair.

'Let me in.'

She adjusted her stance and Scott slipped his fingers between her legs, playing there until she was gasping.

He looked up at her. 'Keep going. I want to see all of you.'

With that, Kate lost any desire for taking things slowly—so much for control!—and reefed the dress up and off. She tossed it to the floor and stood naked before him.

He kept his fingers moving in the moisture between her thighs while he looked up at her. He swallowed again as she pulled her hair back over her shoulders. The movement tightened her breasts, as if she was offering them to him.

His fingers stilled, slipped out of her, and Kate almost protested.

He sat back, eyes all over her. 'You are the sexiest thing I've ever seen,' he said hoarsely, and with a determination that was almost intimidating bent to remove his sneakers.

He got to his feet, reached into his back pocket for a condom, held it out to her.

She took it and instantly started ripping the packet. Scott—with sharp, efficient movements—took off his T-shirt, unzipped his jeans, pushed them and his underwear down and off.

And, God, he was gorgeous. Hard. Huge. Perfect.

He reached for her, pulled her in, groaned long and low as their naked bodies connected, slid together.

'I'm sorry, but this won't take long,' he said. 'We're not going to make it to the bedroom. Not this first time.'

He pulled back, jaw clenched tight. Nodded at the condom in her hand. 'Put that on me and I'll try not to come while you do it.'

Trembling, eager, Kate complied, while Scott uttered a string of low-voiced curses. And then he basically stumbled back, pulling Kate with him, until he was sitting on the chair again.

'Straddle me,' he said. 'I can get more deeply into you from this position. And I want to go deep. Deep and hard. Okay?'

'Okay,' Kate said, in a breathy voice she hardly recognised as her own.

She slid onto his lap, wrapped her legs around him, around the chair. He held her hips, settling her, then shifted so her bottom was in his hands, manipulating her so she was more perfectly positioned for his entry. Another groan, this time against her neck, followed by a sucking kiss there. Then, with one almost vicious thrust, Scott was inside her, pulling her closer, closer. Another sucking kiss on her neck and then his mouth was on hers, kissing her deeply, tongue plunging within, licking her top lip, back inside her mouth.

'Best—the best ever—to be inside you,' he said against her lips.

And somehow those not very romantic words pushed Kate over the edge and into orgasm. She grabbed his face. Pulled his mouth closer, too close for words, and fed him gasping kisses until he followed her, with one long, last, deep thrust, into an explosive orgasm.

Best. Ever.

Those two small words were all Scott could think of as he came back to earth after the most mind-blowing release of his life.

Kate. So jaw-droppingly sexy. Looks that were almost taunting, they were so hot. She'd met him thrust for thrust, taken him as deep and as hard as he wanted to go, kissed the wits right out of his head.

He snuggled her close for a long, quiet moment, stroking her hair gently now that the first rampage of lust had passed. He felt her heartbeats and his, in unison, starting to slow. But he figured he'd never have a normal heartbeat around Kate. She fired his blood like nothing he'd ever experienced. Everyone else he'd ever been with paled in comparison. Every other one was a girl. But Kate was a woman.

And, for now at least, *his* woman.

At the thought, he felt himself start to harden again, still inside her.

She laughed, low and deep. She'd felt that, then.

She pulled back and looked into his eyes. Kissed him again, lush and soft, and he got harder still.

He stood, bringing Kate with him. Her legs wrapped automatically around him.

'Bedroom's back there,' she said with a head movement.

'I hope it's a single,' he said with a laugh as she squirmed against him. 'Because anything wider than that is going to be a waste of space.'

* * *

Three hours later Scott got quietly out of Kate's bed, pulled on his jeans and T-shirt, and looked down at her.

She was deeply asleep, no doubt exhausted after what he'd put her through. Even when he hadn't been able to get it up after that third time he hadn't stopped touching her. Mouth, hands…all over her.

Best. Sex. Ever.

He thought about leaving and going home—but that felt… wrong. Sneaking away as though he'd got what he came for and didn't have to linger. Not that Kate would mind, given the contract. Sex—just sex. The end-game. He could sneak away and it wouldn't be regarded as sneaking by either of them.

But they hadn't had dinner and he was too hungry to leave. She would be too if she woke before morning. He padded into the kitchen, checking the contents of the cupboards and fridge. Not overly stocked, but he could fix omelettes.

Making himself at home—as he always seemed to do in kitchens—Scott got busy with eggs and whisk and was soon sliding his perfectly cooked omelette onto a plate. He grabbed a glass of wine—making a mental note to bring some beer to leave in Kate's fridge—and pondered where he should sit to eat.

But it was no contest—and he knew it in his heart.

He'd said earlier that he wasn't interested in the view from Kate's apartment. And in that first hot burst of screaming desire it had been true—she was the only thing of interest to him.

But he knew what the view was, and now that the edge had been taken off his caveman libido he wanted to see it.

Rushcutters Marina, where he'd boarded his first yacht as a child and learned to sail. Sailing had become a passion. His one and only rebellion had been taking that year to sail in the Whitsundays rather than go straight to university the way his parents wanted, the way his perfect, by-the-book brother had. For Scott, sailing had been…*freedom*. And even though he'd given up sailing, there was something about boats that just kept pulling at him.

So he settled himself at Kate's girl-sized outdoor table and looked out at the water as he ate. It should have been peaceful but, as ever, he found peace elusive.

He finished his omelette and walked over to the edge of the terrace, looking out at the water, listening to the gentle lap of it against the boats.

It was so different from the Whitsundays, and yet it made him remember that time eight years ago at Weeping Reef. The six of them—Willa, Luke, Amy, Chantal, Brodie and him—had formed what they'd imagined would be a lifelong bond, when their lives had been just beginning, only to see that bond disintegrate before that one summer was over.

All because of a love triangle.

One moment Chantal was Scott's girl; the next she was Brodie's. No words needed. Because everyone had been able to see it, just from the way they'd looked at each other.

Brodie was the only person Scott had ever confided in about all his childhood crap—and it had been hard to deal with his best friend slipping straight into the place his brother usually occupied in his tortured mind: the best, number one. As the white-hot knowledge had hit, Scott had lashed out, and everything had crashed and burned.

Scott and Chantal, both stuck working at Weeping Reef for the summer, had never recovered the friendship that had been between them before they'd become lovers.

Brodie had simply disappeared.

And Scott had missed him every single day. He *still* missed him.

The fight seemed so stupid, looking back. But that was what happened when you combined too many beers and too much unseasoned testosterone.

Chantal was just a girl—albeit it a smart, beautiful, wonderful girl—and what they'd had was a romance of proximity. They'd arrived at the resort before the others, and everyone had automatically assumed they were an item because they looked perfect together. A default relationship. With occasional sex that had been fun but hardly earth-shattering.

The fight hadn't been about Chantal. Scott knew that with hindsight. That fight had been all about *him*. About never being quite good enough to win the prize. Never being quite good enough to *be* the prize.

At least he'd learned from the experience. Learned not to trust. Learned to take control of his emotions and hang on to that control at all costs. Learned to keep his pride intact. Learned not to care too deeply. About friends…or lovers.

Now, if only he could work out how to deal with the restlessness that had followed him ever since, he'd be happy. But it was as if he was in a constant battle with himself: *let go and just be; don't ever let go; let go; don't let go; just be…*

'Couldn't you sleep?'

The soft question from behind him startled him out of his heavy thoughts. Scott took a moment to school his features. And then he turned, dialled up a smile—one that was a little bit naughty, a little bit *sex me up*—which he routinely used on women he'd just laid.

Kate was wearing a loose, light dressing gown, and looked tousled and natural and lovely.

'You wore me out, Katie,' he said. 'I needed fuel, so I made myself an omelette. I'll make one for you too—because if you tell me I didn't wear you out in return, I'll die of shame.'

She chuckled. 'Oh, I'm worn out, I promise. We're equal.'

She came over to stand beside him and he found himself drawing her close, tucking her against his side, under his arm.

'I think that qualifies as a PDA,' Kate said.

'We're not in public, so how can it?'

He felt her sigh at his dodge-master answer but she didn't say anything, so he kept her there, under his arm. It was… restful, somehow.

'I love this view,' she said after a long moment.

'Best harbour in the world.'

'Yes,' she said slowly. 'But it's more about the boats for me. The thought of sailing away from your troubles, beginning a wonderful adventure. The freedom of it. I've often dreamt about stealing a yacht and just going.'

She must have felt the slight jerk he gave, because she turned her face up to his, frowning.

'What?'

'A lawyer? Stealing? *Sacré bleu.*'

Her eyes narrowed. 'Yes, but that's not really it, is it?'

Pause. And then he laughed—even managing to make it sound natural. 'What you said just reminded me of my own sailing adventures, that's all. And not that I want to burst your bubble, but reality will bite you on the arse wherever you are.'

'Ah, of course—I forgot you were a sailing instructor at Weeping Reef. You and the other guy I haven't met yet. Brodie?'

That was all it took for Scott to tense up. Brodie's name coming out of Kate's mouth. He didn't want to talk about Brodie. It was too personal, too…raw. God, *still*.

'So what part of it bit you?' Kate asked.

'Let's just say I was too young to appreciate the experience,' he said, and forced himself to smile down at her. This smile meant *go no further*—and he didn't have to use it often because he didn't let people get close enough to push his buttons.

'And, no,' he added quickly, thinking to nip in the bud any other question she might have brewing, 'that's not an invitation to tell me I'm still too young. I'm old enough to have made the sensible choice: sail back to Sydney, go to university, become an architect. All grown-up—just like you. Now, are you ready for your omelette?'

He could sense her slight hesitancy. Another question…? A comment…? But Kate finally shrugged, smiled. And thankfully gave up.

'How lucky am I?' she said. 'A man who sizzles in bed *and* in the kitchen.'

'I like cooking—the orderliness of it. You put a set number of ingredients together and, as long as you combine them in the right order, they come out at the other end in perfect formation.'

Kate grimaced. 'My cooking doesn't do that!'

'Mine does. I insist on it.'

He leaned down and kissed her.

'No kissing,' Kate said, pulling away awkwardly after a moment. 'Not outside of sex. Remember the rules.'

'Oh, yeah, the rules.'

Well, Scott happened to think parts of her contract were ridiculous, as *well* as not being legally enforceable. So not only was he *not* going to be controlled by her rules, he was going to enjoy flouting them. The kissing clause was a case in point. He liked kissing Kate, so he was going to keep kissing her. Simple.

'You know, Katie, a kiss isn't a declaration of honourable intentions, if that's what's bothering you. I assure you my intentions are still *entirely* dishonourable—so relax. It shouldn't surprise you, as the owner of that sexy-as-hell mouth, that men want to kiss it.'

'But—'

Scott swooped before she could get another word out, kissing her again, drawing from the deep well of expertise he'd amassed during an impressive career of seduction. And this time it took her longer to pull away.

'Scott!'

'Hey, this is pre-contract,' he argued. 'We're still on payback sex, by my reckoning.'

'I owed you one orgasm. And I paid that back on the dining room chair. We're on the clock now—and I can't believe you're blurring the rules on day one.'

'Then if it makes you feel better,' he said, grabbing her hands and pulling her in close, '*this* kiss is going to lead to sex.'

And with that, he lowered his head once more, put his mouth on hers. He felt her melt, melt, melting into him. *That* was control. He would control this. Control *her* through her precious contract. Take what he wanted when he wanted it with a clear conscience and no hard feelings when they said goodbye at the end. He'd finally achieved perfection in a relationship!

Not that this was a relationship.

Scott nudged her legs apart, settled himself between them, thrust against her. 'See? I'm ready for you already.'

'Is that perma-erection of yours a benefit of youth?' she asked, leaning into him.

'I could be a hundred years old and five days dead and still want you, Katie,' he said in return. 'Let's go to bed and I'll show you how much. And *then* I'll make you an omelette before I head home.'

CHAPTER SIX

KATE DIDN'T KNOW if it was youthful vigour or if Scott just had more testosterone than the average man, but he'd been at her apartment nine nights in a row. He'd only skipped the tenth night because he had a pre-scheduled poker night—and he'd bemoaned not being able to get out of *that*!

Each time they'd both been insatiable, from the moment he stepped inside to the moment he staggered out, bleary-eyed, in the wee hours.

By tacit agreement Scott never stayed the night. That would have been too…intimate. And, okay, that seemed ridiculous, given the extent to which they'd examined each other's bodies—she'd seen the kitten-shaped birthmark on Scott's right butt cheek, for God's sake, so cute it hurt—but there was something 'next step' about sleeping together. And the contract didn't allow for next steps.

Their nine encounters had included two Play Times.

The first Play Time Scott had turned up as a doctor making a house call. Doctor/patient had been hilarious, to start with. But it had quickly progressed to hot, hot, hot as he'd gloved up and examined various parts of her body, sounding cool and professional with his 'How does that feel?' and 'Is that helping?' while she squirmed and gasped and orgasmed in a long, crazy, unending stream.

Their second Play Time, on their ninth night together, he'd opted for master/slave—but with a midway role-swap.

For the first part of the evening Kate had been the master. Which was just as well, because her phone had been running so hot she would have made an unsatisfactorily preoccupied sex slave. Her client Rosie was in crisis mode, having finally asked for a divorce, and was calling Kate every fifteen minutes for advice. Another client was desperate for help because his ex-wife was threatening to move interstate with their two children. And a colleague wanted advice on a property settlement.

None of it had seemed to faze Scott, who'd taken to his slave role like a duck to water and lavished attention on her as she'd stressed on the phone. Making her tea, massaging her shoulders and feet, rubbing her back, stroking her hair...

And when the phone had finally stopped ringing he'd reduced her to a state of orgasmic bliss. By which time she'd been *dying* to be his slave and would have agreed to anything he asked.

But Scott had issued only one command: that she accompany him to the Visionary Architect Awards dinner.

Which was how now, two nights later, Kate found herself in her best evening gown—a modernised cheongsam in royal purple satin—her hair pinned into a complicated bun, her face flawlessly made-up, essentials stuffed into a glittery silver evening bag...

And feeling all kinds of weird.

A date that wasn't a date.

With a lover who wasn't a boyfriend.

And, despite her being Scott's 'slave' tonight, he'd insisted on coming to her door to get her, like an old-fashioned gentleman caller.

It was...*confusing*. And Kate knew she wouldn't be any less confused by the end of the night. Because not only was Scott a master manipulator, adept at getting her to do whatever he wanted, he was also a champion question-deflector. If she asked him something he didn't want to answer he would just kiss her! And if she complained about kissing being against the rules he would insist the kiss was going to lead to sex, and the next moment they'd be in bed.

Kate had never had so much sex in her life! Or so few answers.

And the upshot was that she wanted to know...well, *everything*!

She was even insanely curious about what Scott would be wearing tonight—something she'd never, ever contemplated ahead of dates with other men…*not* that this *was* a date. How ridiculous was that? It was a black-tie event: ergo, Scott would be in black tie. No need to be curious because all men looked pretty much the same in black tie.

A thought that went straight out of her head—along with the rest of her grey matter—when she opened the door to him and her heart did a thudding swoon.

He was just *so* gorgeous.

Tux in navy blue. Formal shirt in black, not white. He'd forgone the bow tie. Shoes that were buckled, not laced. He looked modern and edgy and scrumptious. Exactly the way an award-winning architect should look.

'Wow!' she said, after a moment of stunned silence.

'Wow yourself!' he responded, and kissed her. 'I wish I'd come over after the game last night, because now I think I'm suffering withdrawal symptoms. I don't know how I'm going to keep my hands off you during dinner.'

And as Kate's heart swooned again—at the kiss, at his words—she wondered if she could invoke *her* first Play Time and whisk Scott off at some stage of the evening for some restroom sex. And she'd *never* wanted to try that before.

Scott took her hand—hmm, PDA or just giving her some support for her five-inch heels?—and didn't let go until they reached his car. When Kate did a double-take, because it was a red Mini—not at all what she would have expected. Not that she'd given a lot of thought to what car Scott would drive, but shouldn't it be a little less…well, *cute*? A little more macho? Like maybe a black off-road truck. Something that did not remind her that he had a kitten-shaped birthmark she would love to see *right that second*.

Scott opened the car door for her and helped her in before getting behind the wheel.

'I hate these events,' he said as he buckled his seat belt. 'So thank you for not leaving me sad and dateless.'

'I'm your slave, remember? I didn't have a choice.'

'Hey, yeah—I forgot!' he said. 'So in that case I would like a kiss for the road.'

'Your wish…my command,' Kate said, and leaned over to give him a steamy, lingering kiss. Even though that kiss was not going to lead to sex. *Uh-oh.* She was getting as bad as him.

But at least he was looking suitably scorched when she eased back.

'Definitely not going to keep my hands off you during dinner,' Scott said fervently.

Kate laughed. 'Not that I believe for a moment that a phone call to the first name in your little black book wouldn't have snagged you a date.'

'Not wishing to sound like an egomaniac, but that is true. The fidelity clause, however, is a killer,' he said. 'How ungallant it would have been, beating off my lascivious companion at the end of the night.'

'You're not telling me your dates always end in sex?'

'Aren't I?'

Kate dutifully laughed—but the idea of him even thinking about sex with another woman was somehow unsettling. And the fact that it unsettled her was…well, *that* was unsettling too.

'You're the one who got fussy about that fidelity clause,' she reminded him, aiming for a nonchalance she just couldn't make herself feel. 'If it's a hardship to give up all those women out there panting for you, you only have to say the word.'

'I'm not risking you ditching me that fast.'

'Who says I'd ditch you? Maybe I wouldn't care.'

He shot her a curious look. 'You honest-to-God wouldn't have minded if I'd done the deed elsewhere tonight?'

'We'll never know, will we?'

'Yeah—not buying it,' he said. 'You wouldn't have liked it. And—just to remind you—I definitely *would* mind, so no going there for you.' Quick, cheeky grin at her. 'Not that you need to.'

'Oh, the confidence of youth.'

Another grin. 'Not youth—*skill,* Katie. And, for the record, it's not that I couldn't have resisted Anais—she's the first A in my black book, by the way—because I could have. It's that I didn't want to hurt her feelings with a knockback she wouldn't have been expecting. So, you see, you had to come to spare the poor girl's feelings.'

'Oh, so this is all about me doing Anais a favour!'

'Well, you can't deny you've got a soft spot for the oppressed.'

'Has Willa been talking about my imminent canonisation again?'

'Nope. I just know, Saint Kate. When you were on the phone two nights ago I sensed weeping aplenty and a fair amount of teeth-gnashing at the other end of the line—and I heard how you dealt with it.' Scott reached for her hand, brought it to his mouth, kissed it. 'All class.'

Kate, uncharacteristically flustered, had to swallow twice before she could force herself back into banter mode and once more to actually find her voice.

'And poor Anais is oppressed *how*, exactly?' she asked—and was relieved the question had come out light and amused.

'All right, you got me,' Scott said, rueful. 'Anais is not oppressed. In fact, she tried to oppress *me*!'

'You? Oppressed? *Puh-lease*.'

'She *did*! Bondage and discipline. *Ouch*. Evil. I cried like a baby.'

Kate couldn't help it. She laughed. 'So that's what I have to do to keep you in line, is it?'

'No. I told you—I'm not into all that. All you have to do to keep me in line, Katie, is redirect your soft spot where it's needed.'

'And where would that be?'

'Well, to me, obviously. Haven't you been listening? I'm oppressed.'

'You need a little more oppression,' Kate said dryly, and when he laughed, sounding boyish and completely irresistible, she found herself wanting to kiss him again.

She decided a subject-change was required for her own sanity.

'So, what are the chances of Silverston taking the prize tonight?' she asked.

Scott waited a moment. 'Did you look it up?'

'Well, yes, of course. What kind of slave would I be if I didn't know what award my master was up for? Creative Residential. Five finalists.'

'I'm not expecting to win.' He sounded offhand—but his hands had tightened on the steering wheel.

'Why not?' she asked.

A shrug, but no answer. Just one of those smiles that she thought he must have stacked up like a jukebox—pick one and play it.

'I hope the food is good, because I'm starving,' he said. 'What's the bet it'll be smoked salmon out of a packet, followed by overdone steak with three vegetables on the side, then chocolate mousse?'

Which, of course, was not an answer. And it seemed she wasn't going to get one, because Scott kept the conversation flowing around a host of boy subjects—which Kate suspected had been deliberately chosen—for the rest of the drive.

Sports results—*please, kill her*—action movies, gory television shows.

By the time they arrived at the five-star hotel where the event was being held, Scott had a new jukebox smile pasted on—a smile that said *I'm here! No big deal!*

But it became obvious very quickly to Kate that his arrival was, in fact, a *very* big deal—to everyone except him. As pre-event cocktails were served outside the ballroom people made their way to Scott in a steady stream, drawn as though by a magnet. But although Scott smiled, chatted, shook hands, kissed a score of female cheeks, he held everyone at bay…and they didn't even realise he was doing it. He was effortlessly, carelessly charismatic, and people clearly wanted to be in his orbit, but he was essentially untouchable.

What the hell...?

Kate remembered what he'd said that day in her office. *I don't get hurt.* She was starting to believe it was true. To get hurt you had to be close to someone. And dial-a-smile Scott wasn't close. To *anyone.* The question was: why not?

'Bored?' Scott asked her, leaning in close.

'No. Why?'

'You were staring off into space.'

'Oh, just...thinking. But not bored.'

'Well, *I'm* bored. Slave or not, I'm going to have to think up a way to reward you for sacrificing your night to this tedium.'

'Just win the prize,' she said.

Instantly his eyes shuttered. 'Hmmm.'

That was all he said. *Hmmm.*

What the hell...?

'Have the organisers already notified the winners?' Kate asked, puzzled. 'Is that why you're so sure you're not going to win?'

'No. It's not— No.'

'Then...what?'

One of those dismissive shrugs. 'I just don't.'

'Don't what?'

'Win. That's the way it is, Katie.' He looked over her shoulder. 'Ah, the doors are opening. Let's go in and try not to...' His eyes widened, his voice trailed off. Then, 'Damn,' he said under his breath. 'He *is* here.'

Kate turned to see what he was seeing. 'What? Who? Oh! He looks like—'

'Me.'

'Only—'

'Taller.'

'Well, yes, but—'

'Better-looking.'

'I was going to say "older".'

His eyes zoomed to her. 'Are you going to tell me he's more

age-appropriate for a thirty-two-year-old? Because if you are—don't. I'm not up to another discussion about my age.'

Kate could only blink. She seemed to be thinking *What the hell?* a lot tonight but…well, *what the hell…?*

His eyes roamed behind her again. 'Oh, for the love of God!'

Kate turned again as Scott's lookalike descended on them.

'Who *is* he?' she asked.

'My brother. His house is one of the finalists.'

That was all he had time to say before he was enveloped in a bear hug.

'Scottie!' his brother boomed out.

Scott stiffened, before giving his brother an awkward pat on the back.

Edging back as fast as he could, he took Kate's elbow and brought her closer. 'Kate—my brother Hugo.'

Hugo? As in Play Time? The word that would stop Scott in his tracks? *What the freaking hell…?* This evening was turning out to be very…instructive.

The resemblance between the two men wasn't as strong close-up. Hugo was like a more refined version of Scott. His eyes were brown, not green. And he spoke with a slightly British accent—very different from Scott's Aussie drawl. Kate thought the accent was an affectation until Hugo confessed, with the fakest attempt at self-deprecation Kate had ever heard, that he'd been to medical school in England.

He looked more conservative than Scott—from his sharp, perfect haircut to his traditional black-tie get-up. Hugo was more talkative, more…accessible. But there was something missing. That indefinable something Scott had in spades— that mix of charm and wit and sexy intrigue. Hugo was obviously smart. He was good-looking. A little stuffy, maybe, although he seemed like a decent guy. But nobody would rush to Hugo's side the way they rushed to Scott's.

Kate was on the point of filing that description away when Hugo raised the subject of the award, with a look at Scott that could only be described as *pitying*—and Kate's hackles rose, sharp and hard. Okay, description revised. Hugo was *not* a decent guy; Hugo was a bastard.

'So—Creative Residential! Who would have thought we'd end up competing *again*, Scottie?' Hugo asked, with a heavy clap on Scott's back. 'I checked out Silverston on the website. Good job, Scottie. *Really* good job.'

'Thank you,' Scott said with a smile that was definitely forced.

Kate, *hating* that smile, blinked innocently up at Hugo. 'You're not a doctor *and* an architect, are you, Hugo?'

'Well, no, but—'

'So your *architect* is the finalist?' More wide-eyed *I don't understand* innocence.

'Yes, my man Waldo.'

'Oh, your *man*. I see. Scott's client is leaving the honours to him. Credit where it's due, right?' Kate asked, and hoped Scott's client wouldn't embarrass her by appearing out of nowhere!

Hugo chuckled, oblivious to any insult. 'Ah, but I had considerable input into Waldo's design,' he explained. 'So when I asked if I could come along this evening, of course Waldo was only too happy. Especially when I told him there would be a little friendly family rivalry for the prize.'

Scott, whose eyes had frosted in a way that did not look at all friendly, raised his eyebrows. '*Waldo* let you have a say? Waldo *Kubrick*?' He turned to Kate. 'Waldo is brilliant— actually, the best. But he's more temperamental than a busload of French chefs.'

Hugo gave Scott another pitying look. 'Yes, he *is* the best, isn't he?' Then came an apologetic and yet not *at all* apologetic cough. 'Sorry, Scottie.'

'Sorry?' Scott asked. 'Why?'

There was something in Hugo's eyes that Kate didn't like. Something malicious.

'Let's just say Knightley is pretty special,' he said. 'The buzz is there.'

Kate felt a laugh building and had to bite the inside of her cheek hard. Knightley? His house was called *Knightley*?

'Yes, it is,' Scott said coolly, and gestured towards the ballroom. 'Well, good luck, Hugo. We're heading in.'

And then Scott turned to Kate—who was trying not to laugh and at the same time silently communicating to Scott that she knew why the name *Hugo* would stop him in his Play Time tracks—and something lit in his eyes as he took in the expression on her face. And his smile, for the very first time, was in his eyes.

And it was absolutely devastating.

Scott felt a little off-balance.

It had been a lightning-fast emotional shift—from the normal feeling of inadequacy he always experienced around his brother to wanting to take Kate in his arms right there in front of Hugo, to whom he never, ever introduced *anyone*. And not only take her in his arms but breathe her right into his body. All because she'd wanted to laugh. It didn't seem to matter that he didn't even know what had amused her. Not that Kate didn't usually laugh—she did, a lot, and he loved that. But there was just something different about it tonight.

'What's so funny?' he asked as he pulled out her chair.

She sat. Waited for him to sit beside her. 'Not that I want to disparage your brother, *Scottie*—'

He groaned.

'Sorry, but I owe you for all the Katies,' Kate said.

Wince. 'Yeah. I get it. No more Katies. Hand-on-heart promise.'

'But what is *with* that house name? Is Hugo an *Emma* fan? Or maybe his wife? Naming the house after Mr Knightley, perhaps?'

'Emma who?'

Kate rolled her eyes. 'Never mind. I think the explanation is simpler. He named it after *himself*, didn't he? Like one of those British stately homes?' She was biting the inside of her cheek again. 'Maybe he got the idea at med school…'

'Knightley,' Scott said slowly. *Knightley.* Oh, my God. I didn't even think— It never occurred— I mean—God!' He sat, stunned, for a moment, and then he started laughing. *'God!'*

'It's not a laughing matter,' Kate admonished, but Scott could see she was struggling to keep a straight face. 'It's *de rigueur* to name your home after yourself, you know.' Her mouth was starting to twist. 'My own apartment is c-called C-Castle C-Cleary.'

And then Kate was laughing too, and the sound of it was just so sexy he had to touch her. Needed to share this delicious absurdity with her physically.

He reached for her hand and she twined her fingers with his, still laughing. Even her eyes were laughing. What must that be like? To have eyes that laughed? Eyes that were warm like molten silver. Beautiful.

His throat closed over and the laughter jammed. Stuck in his throat. All he could think about was kissing her until she was breathless. As breathless as he felt just looking at her. Breathless. And perfect. For once, perfect…

Kate stopped laughing too, and then she reached out with her free hand. Touched his face as if she felt it too. The connection.

And then panic hit.

No! No connection. He didn't want that.

He jerked back, away from her touch.

He looked at their joined hands, and the sight of their linked fingers jolted him like an electric shock. He let go.

He picked up his wine glass, took an urgent swallow. And then, eyes sliding away to some distant point, he cleared his throat.

Kate cleared her own throat, picked up her own wine glass, sipped. He heard the quick breath she took.

'So…um…what's it like?' she asked, putting the words out hesitantly into the sudden, excruciating void.

Wine. He needed another sip. Took it. Put the glass down. 'What's what like?'

'Knightley?'

Shrug. 'I know as much as you do about Knightley. Just what I've seen on the awards website.' He waved at someone across the room.

'So it must be... Is it...? Is it brand-new, then? I mean that you haven't seen it?'

'No,' he said. 'I just haven't. Seen it, I mean.'

Their first course arrived, and Scott almost sagged with relief. He pasted on a cheerful smile, and at last he could look at her again. 'Well, Kate—as you can see, I was on the money with the smoked salmon.'

From that point the seemingly endless procession of award presentations, cheesy entertainment and bland food courses proceeded exactly as Scott had expected. Except for one thing: a burning awareness of Kate beside him. Something he'd never felt with Anais or any of his other black-bookers at one of these insipid evenings.

And that bothered him.

Even the way she was captivating the architect on her other side was getting to him. Thank God Miles Smithers was sixty years old and happily married, or he'd probably want to smash the guy's tee—

Whoa! Pull up. There was no thanking God required. Or teeth-smashing. It didn't matter if Kate was captivating a sixty-year-old married architect or a thirty-two-year-old billionaire Greek god! If she was physically faithful she could captivate whomever the hell she wanted to captivate. None of his business.

And it wasn't as though he was being a scintillating conversationalist himself. If not for Miles, Kate would be catatonic! He was being a first-class boor, barely grunting a reply when she asked him anything.

All because of that...that moment. That intense connection which he hadn't bargained for and didn't bloody well want.

Having Hugo sitting two tables away, already looking every inch the victor, wasn't helping either.

Scott had known his brother wouldn't be able to stay away tonight, wouldn't be able to vacate the space, just for once, and let Scott occupy it. But he'd been anticipating a hand-wave and a superior nod across the room—that was their usual interaction. It must have been the sight of Kate that had prompted Hugo to dial it up a notch.

Kate. So glamorous and secure and beautiful. Out of his league. Which Hugo would have seen at a glance. So he probably should have guessed Hugo wouldn't have been able to resist coming over in person to foreshadow his win.

And Knightley *would* win.

Because Hugo *always* won, even if he had to win via a third party like Waldo.

When the Creative Residential category was announced Hugo looked directly at him. There was a tiny narrowing of his eyes, an oh-so-poignant smile—a look Scott had being seeing all his life. A look that said *Sorry, I just can't help it that I'm so much better than you, little brother.* Even more insufferable than usual because Kate saw it. And, God, how he wished he could get her out of there so she didn't have to see it again when he lost. Why, why, *why* had he brought her?

Knightley was the second finalist announced. Pictures flashed up on the huge screen at the front of the room and—yes—it was a knockout. Hugo turned to clink glasses with Waldo, who had the grace to look uncomfortable about such precipitate celebration.

Two more finalists.

Then Scott's name was announced. Silverston was being described in admiring detail and Kate turned to him, radiant, looking as if she was proud of him or something. She took his hand in hers as though that were entirely natural, held on.

PDA, Scott wanted to say—but couldn't get it out of his tight throat. This was embarrassing. He wasn't going to win. Kate would be giving him one of Hugo's pitying looks in a minute, and having her hold his hand while she did so would only make it harder to stomach.

He wanted to disengage his hand, but couldn't seem to let go. So he concentrated, instead, on making his hand go slack and dead. Let her interpret that. She'd be letting go of his hand any moment now. Any moment… Any….

Nope.

She wasn't letting go. And everything was starting to blur in his head until he forgot why he shouldn't be holding her hand.

Flashing images on the giant screen… The MC leaning into his microphone, saying something… A short blare of music… Spotlights swirling…

Scott found that, far from going slack and dead, his hand was gripping Kate's. Hers was gripping right back.

And then she leaned in and kissed him briefly on the lips, and he thought, *What?*

And the applause was ringing out.

And the spotlight—it had stopped on him. It was shining on him. On *him*!

He blinked. Shook his head.

Kate laughed. Nodded.

And Scott knew. He'd won. He'd really won.

He was too shocked even to smile, let alone move. But Kate nudged him and somehow he got to his feet, started heading towards the stage—only to realise he was still holding Kate's hand. He looked down at it, looked at her. She was laughing as she raised his hand to her lips, kissed it—the way he'd kissed hers in the car. And he needed exactly that, right at that moment. *Exactly.*

And then he was walking to the front of the room, up onto the stage.

'Wow,' he said when he got to the microphone. 'Like… *wow!* Okay, this is like one of those moments where the award-winner says they never really expected to win…and then pulls out a *just in case* speech.'

General laughter.

Deep breath.

'But I don't have a *just in case* speech. So…so…um… thank you. I mean—to my client, to the team at Urban Sleek. The other finalists! So amazing. And…and Kate. Just…for… well. Thanks again. And…well, wow.'

Trophy in hand, Scott made his way back to the table, where Kate kissed him again, and he sat in a daze for the rest of the presentations, embarrassed at having given the worst speech in the history of all awards ceremonies everywhere in the world. But he'd just never expected to win. Why would he have prepared a speech? He never won. *Never.*

It wasn't until the final award was being presented that he remembered Hugo. He looked over at Hugo's table, saw his empty seat—bathroom visit?—and then forgot all about Hugo as formal proceedings gave way to the dancing and socialising part of the evening and what felt like a horde of people headed over to congratulate him.

He figured Kate must be longing to escape by the time the throng of well-wishers had dissipated, but when he opened his mouth to suggest they make a run for it, she smoothed a hand over his lapel and smiled at him—and his brain cells scrambled.

'Don't you think we should have a celebratory dance?' she asked.

Scott looked from her to the dance floor, then back.

'Scott?' She smiled. 'Dance?'

'Er…'

Really? 'Er…' is the best you've got? Get it together.

Clearing of the throat. 'Actually, I'm not much of a dancer, Kate.'

'That's all right, neither am I.'

'No—I mean I don't. Dance. Ever.'

She seemed startled by that. 'You mean you never *have*?'

He checked his watch. 'I was thinking… It's late. I should get you home. You've suffered enough.'

Kate was watching him. Curious, a little wary. She seemed

on the verge of asking something… But then she gave her head a tiny shake and said, 'Sure.'

Scott was silent on the drive to Kate's. Because the tension he'd been feeling all the way up to the announcement of his win was back. Tenfold. And it must have rubbed off on Kate because she was silent too, staring through the windscreen.

He pulled up outside her building and Kate unbuckled her seat belt. Then she just sat there, looking at him, waiting for him to turn off the ignition.

'Aren't you coming up?' she asked at last.

'I thought…it's late…I thought…'

'*I* thought you said all your dates ended with sex?'

Silence. Awkward.

'Ah, but not tonight,' Kate said. 'Well, we only specified two nights a week, didn't we? And we've hit that target. But, just so you know, slave girl ends now.'

With that throaty laugh he loved a little too much, she opened the car door and got out. But then she leaned down to look in at him. 'Congratulations again, Scott. That was some house you designed.'

'Thanks. And…and…' Shrug. 'Goodnight, Kate.'

Door closed.

Night over.

Thank God.

Scott drove off, up the street, around the corner, heading home.

Ordinarily he would have helped his date out of the car. That was what he always did, because that was the gentlemanly thing.

Ordinarily he would have walked his date to her front door—again, gentlemanly.

Ordinarily he would have followed his date inside, all the way into her bed. Gentlemanly? No. But expected. On both sides.

Ordinarily.

But with Kate…?

Well, it wasn't a *date*.

It was supposed to have been just an easy fix for the night. Because he really *hadn't* felt like going the black-book route and he really *hadn't* wanted to do the sexual brush-off at the end—which he definitely *would* have done, because fidelity really *was* a sticking point for him and he really *wasn't* interested in having sex with anyone except Kate. *For now*, he added, just to be clear on that. And, aside from all of that, it had been fun to manipulate Kate's rules by negotiating her role tonight as part of Play Time.

An easy fix, a non-date, a fun manipulation.

But it had turned into something…*else*.

Because with her there, the award had been somehow more important than it should have been—and that had surprised him.

Because Hugo had tried to show off to her and she hadn't thought he was anything special—in fact, she'd thought he was a little bit ridiculous.

Because they'd laughed together like…like *that*.

Because she'd had to go and get all proud and lovely about his award.

None of which had anything to do with the end-game.

And it was the end-game he wanted—not the something… *else*.

So it was best to re-establish some distance between them before he had sex with Kate again. And as for walking her to her front door…? He just hadn't trusted himself to get that far and no further. Not with her.

Anyway, it wasn't as if she was his responsibility. He didn't have to usher her protectively behind locked doors. She wasn't some vulnerable girl who couldn't take care of herself. She *could* take care of herself. She *wanted* to take care of herself. She'd been arriving home from all kinds of dates—and this wasn't even a date—for years. She'd laughed when he'd insisted on going to her door to pick her up tonight. She hadn't looked at all put out that he wasn't getting out of the car to walk her to her door at the end of the night. She didn't want that kind of attention. She didn't need—

Oh, dammit to hell!

Swearing fluently and comprehensively, Scott did a U-turn and sped back to Kate's. He screeched to a stop, leapt from the car, raced to the apartment block and followed a semi-familiar resident into the building without having to press the intercom. Which was fortuitous, because he had no idea yet what he was going to say to explain his reappearance.

His heart was thumping when he reached Kate's apartment and knocked on her door.

He still had no idea what to say, but he was suddenly so desperate to see her he was happy just to wing it. *So answer... open the door...come on.*

Kate opened the door cautiously.

Well, of course she was cautious! He could have been anyone.

'You shouldn't open the door without knowing who it is,' he said. Yep, he had lost his freaking mind.

Her only response was to raise her eyebrows. God, he loved the way she did that—all haughty and amused.

She was still wearing that stunning dress, but her hair was half down and her feet were bare.

Scott cleared his throat. 'I should have walked you to your door.'

'Why?'

'Because it's the right thing to do.'

She shook her head, laughed as though to say *silly boy*— and that riled him.

So he reached for her, pulled her close and did what he'd been wanting to do all night.

He kissed her.

CHAPTER SEVEN

SCOTT WAS STILL kissing her as he backed her into the apartment and kicked the door closed.

And Kate really wished he didn't have the ability to turn her to mush—because *she'd* wanted to be the one closing the door. *Slamming* it. Right in his face.

Because...because... Well, because how *dared* he make tonight the first date in his life that wasn't ending with sex? *Not* that it was a date, but still!

Pride might have forced her to laugh it off out there in the car, but she was furious. His first date not to end in sex and it was *her*? On *this* night of all nights? An important night he'd *shared* with her? A night when he'd finally shared *something*?

Yep—one hundred per cent furious.

But with Scott kissing her as though he wanted to suck her right into his soul, she felt the anger drain away. Because she could feel that it was more than a kiss. There was something there—something he wanted from her that he couldn't, wouldn't, articulate. Something that made her ache for him, *long* for him.

'Scott, what's wrong?' she asked when he broke away to take a breath. 'Tell me. Please tell me.'

But he kissed her again. 'Just let me...' he said. *Kiss.* 'I want...' *Kiss.* 'I just...'

He didn't finish those sentences. Kate wondered if he'd even finished them in his own head. Because he kept kissing her, for the longest time, as though there *were* no thoughts, just the kissing.

And for tonight, she decided, it was enough.

'Come with me,' Kate said, and led him to the bedroom.

Scott undressed her. First, the cheongsam—falling to the floor in a purple crumple. Next came her underwear. Her most expensive, coffee-coloured silk and lace, removed like an inconvenience. She smiled, remembering the excitement with which she'd donned that underwear, thinking to drive him wild tonight—and now he just didn't care.

He reached into her hair, gently removed the remaining pins, tossed them to the floor. Ran his fingers through the red mass of it, seemingly more interested in her hair than the sight of her naked body.

It felt strange…and thrilling. The way his eyes stayed on her face, her hair.

'Take my clothes off,' he said, and his voice was a throb.

Kate chose first to put her mouth on his, to let it cling there. She took a moment to snuggle against him, feeling both vulnerable and wicked as his arms closed around her and she was held, naked, against his fully clothed body.

Not until he started to shake did she step back, slipping her hands under his jacket, over his shoulders, smoothing it back and off so that it dropped to the floor behind him. Next came his shirt buttons, slipped through their holes as Scott breathed out a long, slow prayer of a breath. Then she eased his cufflinks out.

They looked expensive, so she glanced towards her dressing table, thinking to put them somewhere safe—but Scott stopped her before she could step away.

'Don't leave,' he said.

'But I only—'

He took the cufflinks from her and tossed them over his shoulder as though they were no more valuable than her hairpins. He didn't even blink as they hit the wall.

Kate slid the shirt from his body, stopped to kiss him again, her breasts against his chest, almost moaning at how wonderful that felt.

Next, she undid his pants. Eased them down. Knelt at his feet, unbuckled his shoes. She paused, rose on her knees.

Perfect position for taking him in her mouth. She wanted to do that so badly.

But Scott, reading her mind, drew her up. 'Not tonight,' he said.

A minute later his shoes were off, his pants and underwear kicked away, and she was back in his arms, being held against him, while his hands smoothed down her back, over and over, as he breathed her in, his mouth against her hair. 'Kate…' he said. 'Kate.'

But Kate didn't think he even knew he was saying her name. He seemed to be in a kind of trance.

So she let him lead her to the bed, let him pull the covers back, draw her gently down beside him. He kissed her again, so softly. And then he eased slowly back, taking Kate with him. Wrapped her in his arms. Kissed her eyelids, her mouth, her neck, nuzzled into her hair.

She simply held him, opening to him in any way he wanted. Even the simple act of sliding a condom onto him, his hands lightly covering hers while she did it, seemed like a sensual discovery.

And when at last he positioned her beneath him and slid inside her welcoming heat, it was as though his body sighed and relaxed and just…*was*. For the longest moment he stayed still, taking her face between his hands, laying his mouth on hers, kissing her with an intensity that pierced through to her burning heart.

Tears started to Kate's eyes and she didn't even know why. She closed her eyes, knowing it would change things if he saw her cry. And she wouldn't have changed this slow, sweet loving for anything.

She knew what was happening, and she wanted it. She was giving herself to him: *I'm here, yours.*

His. For tonight she was his. And Scott was hers. Hers alone. For tonight.

And when he spilled himself inside her, with a gasping, luscious groan into the mouth he was kissing so deeply, Kate held him tight, so tightly against her, and wrapped her legs around him, let herself join him in her own flowering release.

'Thank you,' he whispered into her ear.

For what? she wanted to ask, but she dared not break the spell by seeking answers he wouldn't give.

And in any case Scott was holding her close, kissing the top of her head, stroking her back. And it really was enough.

So beautiful… Soothing… Lovely…

Ahhhh…

When Kate woke early the next morning she turned, smiling, to face Scott—only to find his side of the bed empty.

A quick walk through the apartment showed that all he'd left behind was a note, on the kitchen bench.

Saturday night?
S

Two words. One question mark. One initial.

Which brought home to Kate that last night had been just…well, just last night.

He hadn't stayed until morning, the way she'd thought he might. She wouldn't see him tonight, the way she'd hoped. And their relationship hadn't metamorphosed into anything other than what it was: contractual sex.

Which brought her to Saturday night. Yes or no?

She sighed as she looked at the calendar on her fridge. Today was Friday the thirteenth—hopefully that wasn't an omen!—and Saturday, tomorrow, was…

Oh.

Ohhhhh.

Saturday. The fourteenth of February.

Not that the momentousness of that date would have entered Scott's head. He wasn't a Valentine's Day kind of guy.

And in this instance it was a moot point. Because her sister Shay, and Shay's partner Rick—who *were* Valentine's Day kind of people—were leaving their two gorgeous daughters with Kate while they went out for a romantic dinner.

So she should just get straight on the phone and tell Scott she was busy on Saturday. No need to embarrass herself by mentioning Valentine's Day. She didn't want him to think she was angling for something other than sex. Something like... Well, something Valentine-ish.

Even if she had a lump in her throat about the whole stupid day.

A lump so big it was physically impossible to get a word out of her clogged-up throat. Which made a phone call impossible.

Okay, she would email.

Got your note, Scott.
I'm babysitting my nieces, Maeve and Molly, on Saturday night. I'm free Sunday if that suits?
Kate

There. Cool, businesslike. Contract-worthy.

Three hours later, back came a two-word response: No problem.

And Kate released a big, sighing breath.

Right.

Good.

Good...right?

Because Valentine's Day actually sucked. If Kate had a dollar for every now-divorced couple who'd managed either their proposal or their actual wedding on February the fourteenth, she'd be retired already! Valentine's Day was all about spending too much on wilted roses and eating overpriced restaurant dinners.

Stupid.

The worst possible day for scheduling a date with a sex-only partner.

Valentine's Day? *As if!*

Kate went to her kitchen, looked again at the calendar stuck on her fridge.

Yep, there it was. February the fourteenth. With a nice big red heart on it, courtesy of whoever printed stupid refrigerator calendars. A big red heart. A *love* heart.

And, to her absolute horror, Kate's eyes filled with tears.

Kate had a hectic day of meetings, followed by a catch-up with the girls for drinks after work, and by the time she clambered into bed that night, she was sure she was over the whole weepy Valentine's Day phenomenon that had blindsided her.

So when she woke on Saturday morning to find that depression had settled over her like a damp quilt, she went the whole tortured-groan route. What had happened to her brain during that awards dinner on Thursday night to have resulted in her losing all her common sense?

Sex-only partners *did not celebrate Valentine's Day*. Sex-only partners scheduled sex on days like the *fifteenth* of February. A perfectly legitimate, much more appropriate day for having no-strings sex with guys who left two-word notes on your kitchen counter.

A *two-word* note. And a *two-word* email. That encapsulated her relationship with Scott very nicely—two words: *sex contract.*

Imbued with a burst of *damn your eyes* energy, Kate got out of bed and on the spot decided to clean her apartment. An activity that was *not* some kind of displacement therapy twisted up in her need to wash that man right out of her hair, but a simple household activity. A spring clean—just in summer.

She got underway with gusto.

Gusto that lasted approximately fifteen minutes.

Which was how long it took for the first memory to sneak in.

Kate was wiping down the dining table—and there in her head was the memory of that first night…Scott reaching across to hold her breast…and then the whole dining chair thing. *Ohhhhhhh.*

It was like a switch, throwing open the floodgates—because the memories started pouring in, room by room, after that. Plumping up the couch cushions—that night when he'd thrown the cushions off and dragged her on top of him… Cleaning out the fridge—Scott, coming up behind her, hands all over her… Bathroom—three separate shower scenes.

Her bedroom—*holy hell.* So vivid it was painful. And the most painful of all that last time… Scott drawing her gently down onto the bed…kissing her as if he wanted them to merge.

Okay, enough cleaning.

She hurried to the laundry to dump the housekeeping paraphernalia, only to be hit by another memory. *Oh. My. God.* Had she—? Yes, she had! She'd had sex with Scott Knight in *every single room* of her apartment—*including* the damned laundry room! What normal person had sex in the laundry room? Sitting on top of the washing machine, with the vibrations adding a little extra hum to proceedings as you wrapped your legs around—

Arrrggghh.

She had to get out of the apartment. Maybe even *sell* the apartment.

She took a cold shower, changed into *I am not in need of antidepressants* clothes and hurried out of the building.

The boats were what she needed. Up close and personal. Escape. So she crossed the road to the marina and breathed out a sigh of relief as she reached the jetty. The boats would float her stress away as they always did—on a tide of dreams. Adventure. Possibilities.

One day she would hire a sailing instructor and she would learn… She would learn…

Uh-oh.

Her eyes darted from yacht to yacht…and on every deck she could picture Scott Knight eight years ago, young and free, teaching people to sail. Scott as he was now, teaching *her* to sail.

One of those now-familiar tortured groans was ripped out of her and she turned her back on the boats.

Coffee—she needed coffee.

She hurried to the marina cafe and was horrified when Dean the barista's eyes popped at her as if she was a crazy person. 'You okay, Kate?'

What the hell did she *look* like?

'Fine, fine, fine,' she said reassuringly—before realising that two more 'fines' than were strictly necessary did not denote 'fine'. 'I just need coffee, Dean.'

'Really? Because you seem a little wired.'

Forced smile. 'Really, Dean. Just the coffee.' Subtext: *Give me the damned coffee and shut up.*

But as she took her coffee to one of the tables and sipped, Dean kept giving her concerned glances from behind the coffee machine. As if she had a neon sign flashing on her forehead: *Beware of woman losing her marbles.* Thank heaven her coffee of choice was a nice little macchiato. If she'd had to put up with a cappuccino's worth of *Are you okay?* looks she might have gone over and slapped Dean!

As it was, she could chug it down quickly and flee back to her apartment. Where she would look up the official definition of 'pathetic'! Just to be sure she *wasn't.*

Fifteen minutes later she had the dictionary open, her finger running down the column…*paternalism…paternity… paternoster…*

Aha!

Pathetic: arousing pity, especially through vulnerability or sadness.

In other words, *Kate Cleary: sexless on Valentine's Day.* The usually imperturbable Dean, the barista, had instantly clocked her out-of-character vulnerability. And she didn't need a dictionary to know that she was arousing pity—in *herself*!

How very...well, *pathetic*.

Although at least she could dispute the 'sad' part of the definition. Because she was not *sad*. She was sexually frustrated! Completely different from sad. Not that two whole nights without sex was going to kill her. She'd gone way longer than two nights before! *Waaaaaay* longer. She wasn't a nymphomaniac! Or...hell! *Was* she a nymphomaniac?

Nylon...nymph...nymphalid...nymphette... Nymphette? Good Lord—nymphette? *Nympholepsy...*

Nymphomaniac: a woman who has abnormally excessive and uncontrollable sexual desire.

Ohhh, crap. Maybe she *was* a nymphomaniac. At her age! That was just...sad.

Oh, God! Sad!

She was a fully-fledged pathetic nymphomaniac.

Kate fled to the terrace—the only place in the apartment she hadn't had sex with Scott. And the only reason she hadn't had sex with him on the terrace was because exhibitionism wasn't exactly his 'thing'. And, even though it wasn't her 'thing' either, the realisation that she probably would have gone there, *in full view of any passersby*, flashed through her mind and shocked her.

Depraved pathetic nymphomaniac! That was her. And it was Scott Knight's fault. Because she'd never been this desperate for sex in her whole life.

And now she wouldn't even be able to enjoy the view from her terrace, because one quick look at the boats confirmed that Scott was now firmly entrenched as part of her escape daydream.

When the intercom finally buzzed that evening and she heard her sister's calm voice, she almost cried with relief.

Her family always anchored her. And you *had* to get it to-gether when you had two children to entertain.

When Shay and Rick had left she pushed the coffee table out of the way so the girls could take up their preferred posi-tions on the rug—seven-year-old Maeve leaning back against the base of the couch, engrossed in a book about cake and cookie decorating, and five-year-old Molly stretched out on her stomach, leaning on an elbow and drawing her version of a fairy house in her sketchbook.

Kate was just about to pick up the phone to order pizza—the girls' favourite meal—when the intercom buzzed again. Shay and Rick should be sipping champagne at the restau-rant and surely could have telephoned if they were having a last-minute panic—but nobody needed to tell a family law-yer that parents could be irrational!

She pushed the 'talk' button. 'Yes, Shay?' she said with an exasperated laugh.

'Um…nope. It's me, Kate.'

CHAPTER EIGHT

SCOTT.

Kate's vocal cords froze. *God help me, God help me, God help me.*

'Kate? Come on—buzz me up. My arms are going to fall off in a minute.'

Kate buzzed the door and then just stared at it, paralysed.

Something was swelling in her chest—a mixture of joy and yearning and uncertainty. What did it mean that he'd come when she'd told him not to? He shouldn't be doing this. She was glad he was here. No, she wasn't—because they had rules. But it was Valentine's Day. No, that meant nothing. She couldn't let him get away with breaking the rules. No matter how glad she was that he was doing it.

Mmm-hmm. She sure was making a lot of sense!

She heard Scott's voice vibrating through her door like a tuning fork. That disarmingly lazy drawl, addressed to some stranger. A laugh. Yep—he'd hooked a new fan in under a minute.

She rested her palms against the door, could almost *feel* him through it.

Breathe. Just breathe.

One knock.

Breathe!

She opened the door and Scott stepped over the threshold as though he owned the place.

'What are you doing here?' she managed to get out.

'Why wouldn't I be here?'

He handed her two bottles of wine—a white and a red—and carried a six-pack of beer and a paper bag containing who knew what into the kitchen.

Kate followed him, put the red wine on the counter, the white wine and beer in the fridge.

'You can't just buzz the intercom whenever you feel like it,' she said, in her *Don't disturb the children* voice.

Scott shrugged. 'If the intercom annoys you, give me a key.'

Which, of course, was *not the point*. 'I am *not* giving you a key.'

Another one of those shrugs of his. 'Then it's the intercom.'

'You can't stay,' she said. 'I'm just about to order pizza.'

'I love pizza.'

'Not for you, Scott. You shouldn't be here. I told you I was babysitting Maeve and Molly tonight.'

'And I emailed you back to say that wasn't a problem.'

'That wasn't—? I mean... Huh?'

'Oh,' he said. 'Were you trying to tell me not to come? Tsk, tsk, Kate—you have to be more specific, in that case. Lawyers shouldn't be leaving loopholes. So, to be clear...it's not a problem that you're babysitting tonight, which is why I'm here. And, yes, Sunday is fine too.'

Kate thought back to her email, his reply, acknowledged the ambiguity...but knew very well he was playing her.

'You knew what I meant, Scott. And we're supposed to negotiate if we have a problem with dates.'

'Okay, let's negotiate.'

She closed her eyes, took a deep breath. Opened her eyes to find him looking all woebegone.

'Don't you like me any more?' he asked.

She stared at him as laughter and frustration warred inside her. 'No.'

'But why?'

'Because you're—' She broke off, laughed because she just couldn't help it, damn him. 'Just because. And I hope you like entertaining children—because that's the only action you're getting tonight. I can't—won't—leave two little girls eating pizza while you and I go for a quickie in the bedroom.'

He leaned in close, snatched a kiss. 'One—that's just a kiss, not a proposal of marriage, so don't complain. Two—I'm not *asking* you for a quickie in the bedroom while the girls eat pizza. And three—it won't be quick; it will be nice and slow...*after* Maeve and Molly's parents have picked them up.'

One more rapid-fire kiss.

'You really have the most sensational mouth in the world.' Another kiss—quick and scorching. 'And make mine pepperoni.'

He had the nerve to laugh at the tortured look on her face.

'What? Is it the money? I'll pay you half, as per our contract, if that's what's worrying you. Honestly—you lawyers are so tight!'

And with that, he liberated three red foil-wrapped chocolate hearts from the paper bag and presented one to her. 'Happy Valentine's Day.'

And there she went—crumbling. 'Oh, you...you *know* it's Valentine's Day?'

'Well, *yeeeaah*! Multiple cards. Even one present—a cute little cat o' nine tails from Anais that you and I will *not* be trying out. But nothing—*nada!*—from you. And, Kate, I'm warning you—if you haven't had the common decency to buy me a chocolate or a cupcake or at the very least a soppy card, I'm eating half of that chocolate heart.' Quick unholy grin. 'And I'll take mine molten...off your tummy.'

And with that gobsmacking pronouncement, Scott swaggered into the living room while the last of her resistance disintegrated.

'Which one's Maeve and which one's Molly?' he asked. 'No, don't tell me. My friend Willa told me Maeve is seven, so that would be...you.' He pointed to Molly, who giggled. He did an over-the-top double-take. 'Not you?'

Head-shake from Molly.

'I'm Maeve,' Maeve said, and Scott plonked himself down on the rug and leaned back against the couch next to her.

'Okay—will you be my Valentine?' he asked and handed over one of the hearts.

Her eyes lit as she shyly took the heart and nodded.

'Ohhhhh!' That came from the rug. 'What about me?'

Scott nodded sagely at Molly. 'Well, it just so happens I'm in the market for two Valentines tonight.' He produced the other chocolate heart and a beaming Molly came over for long enough to take it from him and give him a sweet little hug before she resettled on the rug.

He turned to Maeve. 'So, Maeve, what's so interesting?'

Maeve flashed her book's cover.

'Ah, you're going to be a chef,' he said.

Maeve nodded, still shy.

'I'm not bad in the kitchen myself,' Scott said, and proceeded to talk about biscuits.

Biscuits? That was just so…random. Biscuits! And chocolate hearts on Valentine's Day. And asking Willa about the girls. Kate didn't know what to make of it all. What to make of *him*.

Unless it was that he was completely irresistible.

She called for pizza, then set the dining table, while Scott charmed her nieces—looking absolutely nothing *like* a confirmed bachelor as he did it.

The man knew his baking. The pros and cons of shortbread, ginger snaps, honey jumbles, chocolate chip cookies and macaroons were all discussed at length. And the absolute deliciousness of…what?…whoopie pies?…was being extolled? Kate had never heard of a whoopie pie.

'They're like little chocolate cookie sandwiches, with a creamy filling,' Scott explained to Maeve—who'd never heard of them either. 'Next time you're here, we'll bake them together.'

'Can I bake too?' Molly asked.

'You sure can. Three of us can make three times the pies! What have you got there, Molly?'

In no time Scott was lying next to Molly on the floor, having the picture explained to him. Maeve abandoned her book to lie on Scott's other side.

Scott gave a bit of improvement advice, explaining that it was his job to design houses, and as Kate paid for the pizzas she heard the girls asking him to redraw the house for them.

'I'd be honoured,' Scott said, and then got to his feet and helped the girls up. 'But first—pizza!'

It was adorable the way he got the girls drinks, helped them choose the biggest pizza slices, chatted about the most beautiful houses he'd designed in a way that made them sound like magic castles. After dinner he stayed with Maeve and Molly while Kate cleared up, drawing in Molly's sketchbook and making the girls *ooh* and *ahh*.

Yep, bona fide adorable.

And Kate just *had* to see the drawing. So she peeked over Scott's shoulder.

Oh. *Ohhhhh.*

It was the perfect little girls' house. Towers and turrets. Winding paths. A secret entrance to an underground treasure cave, a private elf garden, a sunken pool with a waterfall. He'd sketched two bedrooms, labelled 'Molly' and 'Maeve', with fairytale beds and magic mirrors and spiralling staircases.

When Kate took the girls off to clean their teeth and get ready for bed, each of the girls kissed Scott goodnight—one per cheek—and he blushed.

Scott Knight, who could talk more boldly about sex than any man she'd ever met, *blushed.*

Kate felt her heart do one of those swoons inside her chest, and thought, *Uh-oh. This is bad. Very, very bad.*

She read to Maeve and Molly until they drifted into sleep, and then—a little apprehensive—went to find Scott.

He was on the terrace, where he gravitated every time she left him alone.

'I poured you a glass of wine. It's there on the table. And sorry, Kate, but that table's going to have to go, along with the chairs,' he said. 'It's so fragile I feel like I'm going to break something every time I'm near that furniture.'

She had to agree it looked like a children's toy set next to Scott's imposing frame. Everything did. But she forbore from pointing out that she was not going to change her furniture for a man who wouldn't be in her life for long.

Whew. That hit her. This was finite. It had a start date and it would come to an end. She couldn't let herself forget that just because he'd smiled at her once as if he saw something wonderful in her. Or because he'd made love to her once as if he was embedding himself inside her.

Scott took a long pull of beer from the bottle in his hand, gazing out at the marina as Kate fetched her glass and joined him at the edge of the terrace.

'What's it like? Sailing?' she asked.

'It was fun.'

'Was?'

'I don't sail any more.'

'But…why? I mean, why not?'

'It was just…' Shrug. 'Time to concentrate on the important things in life.'

'Fun is important.'

He looked down at her. 'I *am* having fun. With you,' he said, and leaned down to kiss her.

'I know why you do that,' she said, when he pulled back.

'Do what?'

'Kiss me.'

'Well, *duh*, Kate! I do it because I like kissing you.'

'You do it to distract me. So you don't have to answer my questions.'

'And does it? Distract you?'

'Yes. But why are such simple questions a problem for you?'

Pause. 'Prying into my past is not part of the deal, Kate.'

Kate felt it like a slap—not just the words but the *keep your distance* tone. She found she was gripping her glass too hard, so put it on the broad top of the terrace railing.

She heard Scott sigh. Then he was smoothing his hand over her hair like an apology. 'Kate, the sailing... It's just something I set aside to focus on the realities of life—like studying and working. And look at me now—I'm an award-winner!' Low laugh, with all the self-deprecation his brother lacked. 'It's enough for me.'

'If it were enough you wouldn't spend every moment I leave you alone out on the terrace, watching the boats.'

'Pry-ing...' he sing-songed.

'It's not prying to ask questions about a person you... you're...'

'Having sex with,' he supplied. And sighed again. 'You drew up the contract, Kate. There wasn't a clause for fireside chats in there.' Slight pause. 'Right?'

'Right.'

'So has anything changed for you?'

She wanted to say yes. That things *had* changed. Because of the way they'd made love two nights ago. The way he'd presented her with a chocolate heart. And blushed when two little girls had kissed him. The way he tried to pretend that the boats bobbing on the harbour held no fascination for him when she knew they did.

But if things changed he would go. She knew it instinctively. *Not yet. Not...yet.*

'No,' she said quietly, and picked up her wine glass, sipped. 'Nothing's changed.'

They stood in silence, side by side, staring across at the dark water, the city lights in the distance.

And then Scott cleared his throat. Just a tiny sound. 'Good. Because the whole fireside-chat thing... It would be like me asking you...' Shrug. 'I don't know...' Shrug. 'If you wanted...maybe...to have children. One day, I mean.'

Another clearing of the throat. 'Because you're so good with the girls anyone would wonder about that.'

What the hell? Kate slanted a look at him. He was looking out at the Harbour.

But then he turned, looked at her. Eyes watchful. 'And you wouldn't want me to ask you that, would you?'

'If you wanted to ask me that, Scott, I'd answer. Because it's no big deal.'

'Ah, but I don't need to ask. I already know the answer is yes.'

And for the first time in a long time, Kate thought, *Yes.* The answer, very simply, *was* yes. Except of course she'd lost that simple answer somewhere along her career path.

She turned back to the boats. Long moment.

'You know, Scott, I've seen fathers who say they've been tricked into pregnancy and shouldn't have to pay child support. Divorcing parents using child custody as carrot and stick to punish or bribe. Surrogates who decide to keep their children when those children are the last hope of desperate couples. Fathers pulling out all the stops to avoid their children being aborted. Twins separated and fostered because of financial pressure. Unwanted children, abused children, ignored children. I'm not sure that's an enticement to parenthood.'

'But you wouldn't be like any of those parents.'

'No. But a lot of women are good at choosing the wrong man.'

'Then don't choose the wrong man.'

'Oh, simple!' She turned to him. 'So simple that I suppose if you found the right woman it would be a case of *Bingo, let me impregnate you immediately!*'

He laughed softly. 'Since the longest I've been with a woman is two months, I'd say I'm hardly father material.'

Two months. The equivalent of one contract rollover. *Consider yourself warned, Kate.*

'Well, at least you've got the uncle routine down pat,'

she said. 'Judging by how you were with Maeve and Molly.
Where did you learn that? Does Hugo have children?'

'Yes, he does. One girl. One boy. Twins. A perfect set.
My brother does all things to perfection.'

Kate caught the wryness—but before she could even wonder at it Scott had tugged her under his arm, leaned down for
another *that's enough talking* kiss.

'I can't wait to touch you,' he said.

'You *are* touching me,' she said, all breathless—because
that was what it did to her every time he kissed her.

'I'm calling another Play Time next week, Kate.'

'What do you want to do?'

'Uh-uh. Secret. But you're not keeping up. Come on—
don't you have a fantasy *you* want to try out? I'd love to in-
dulge you.'

'I do have something in mind for next week,' Kate said,
because since it was a damned sex contract, and she'd put
that stupid clause in there herself, it would look strange if
she didn't have even one scenario in mind. But the truth was
she could think of nothing she wanted more than just taking
him into her body, holding him close.

'Woo-hoo, I'll be hanging out for that,' Scott said. 'But
remember—no S&M, no B&D. I wasn't kidding about that
stuff. It creeps me out, the pain thing. I don't enjoy it, and
I sure as hell can't see myself inflicting it on you. Oh—
and while fruit and veg is acceptable, under certain circumstances, no wildlife, no livestock. I'm not *that* kinky.'

'Wildlife?' Kate spluttered out a laugh. 'That is just dis-
gusting. Is your black book annotated? Because maybe I'd
better take a look at what you expect. I might have to rein
you in.'

Scott grinned at her. 'Just making sure we're on the same
page after seeing the way that guy in your boardroom was
patting and kissing his little dog like it was his girlfriend.'

Another spluttered laugh. 'Please! You're going to give
me nightmares. And Sugarplum isn't a dog. She's a shih tzu.'

'The dog is called *Sugarplum*?'

'Yep.'

'Well, *that* is an abomination.'

Kate bit the inside of her cheek. 'Actually, I have another name for her. *Hostis humani generis.*'

'Is that a legal term?'

'It is. It means "enemy of the human race". Which I think is very apt in Sugarplum's case.'

'I'm going to have to kiss you for that. Because legal terms get me so damned *hot*! Can you say something with *functus officio* in it?'

She was laughing helplessly. 'Not offhand, no.'

'Then *hostis humani generis* it is.'

Kate was still laughing as Scott planted his mouth on hers…but not for long. By the time he slipped his tongue inside her mouth, she was tingly and dazed. And Scott seemed equally affected.

'I love kissing you,' he breathed against her lips.

'People do tend to love doing things they're particularly good at.'

'You're no slouch yourself—but even if you were, Kate, one look at your mouth is all I'd ever need to get me ready to dive inside you.'

She shivered. Closed her eyes briefly. He could turn her on too easily. So easily it was dangerous.

Change the subject.

'Anyway, Sugarplum's family is sorted. You won't be seeing her around the office again.'

'Who ended up getting the kids?'

'Kids?' Kate asked.

'That couple. You know—the kids?'

'Ah,' Kate said, and winced.

'Not kids?'

Another wince.

'You're not telling me that fight was about that evil little yapper, are you?'

She could see the horror—almost comical and yet not. The disbelief.

Kate shrugged.

'So they don't have kids?' he asked.

'I'm not saying that.'

'So they *do* have kids, but the fight was over…' Stop, stare. 'You're not serious?' he said.

She raised her eyebrows.

He shook his head, stunned. 'I hope they're paying you a lot, because from where I'm standing your job sucks.'

'Lately…yeah, it *does* suck.'

'At least your family must be proud of you, though. Lawyers are like doctors—they've got the parental-pride market cornered.'

'Actually, my mother would probably prefer an architect to a lawyer! She's an artist, so creative stuff is more her speed.'

'Your mother's an artist?' And then his eyes widened. 'Oh! *Ohh!* Cleary! *Madeline* Cleary? Yes! Of course! The painting in your office and the one in your bedroom. Wow.'

'Yes—wow. And my father is a playwright, but not as well known. What about *your* parents?'

'Doctors times two. So…your mother… She's not happy about you being a lawyer?'

'She thinks I get too emotionally invested in my cases. Whenever I stress out, she says, *"Kaaaaate, I warned you how it would be."* And then she adds something about thanking heaven for divorce—which is her way of telling me I'm doing the world a favour, and to just get on with the next uncoupling. It's the Cleary way, you know—fight like hell, then move on.'

'Now, you see, *my* mother would see divorce as an admission of failure. Which is why Knights don't divorce. Failure is not an option.'

'Even if the alternative is to stick with someone who's horrible? Someone abusive? Divorce has got to be a better alternative.'

'Then why do you stress out about it, Kate?'

'I've just…' She paused, sighed. 'I've had a run of nasty ones lately. And seeing people ripping each other apart, seeing the kids on the sidelines…' Another pause. 'It can make you cynical.'

'Cynical. Now, *that* I understand.'

'Which is when I start thinking about boat theft.'

'I'm surprised you haven't done it already.'

'Maybe I would have—except for one small thing.' She slanted him a glinting smile. 'I can't sail!'

He touched her face. Gentle, soft. 'Ah, well—definitely a problem!'

'And, you know, my job has compensations.'

'Money?'

'Yes, that's one.'

'And meeting handsome architects through your clients.'

'Handsome *egomaniacal* architects, even,' Kate said, and laughed. 'But I'd definitely classify meeting Willa as compensation. It was…*satisfying* to fight for her.'

'Yeah, I get that. From what I know of Wayne-the-Pain, he would have tried to screw her out of everything just to pay her back for wanting to be something more than an arm bauble. She said you fought like a demon. That it was your way—to fight to the death.'

'Yes, like I said—the Cleary way. And definitely *my* way. Even more so for people I love—and I love Willa. She's… special. Strong. So much tougher than people think. I admire her more than I can say. She deserves everything good and fine in the world. Joy. Peace. Security. And love. She deserves love.'

'I think you're a secret romantic, Kate.' He nudged her playfully. 'So where's my Valentine's Day card?'

'It's in the mail,' Kate said, nudging him back. 'Along with a few tools of oppression—handcuffs and hot wax to go with Anais's whip, because I think she's on to something there.'

Scott gave an exaggerated shudder. 'I promise you, she

is *not*.' Pause. 'Mind you, for a B&D aficionado, Anais has some remarkably pedestrian notions about love.'

'What's pedestrian?'

'Let's just say the idea of a straight up and down sex contract would never have entered her head. You and I… We're… *different*. We know what we want and what we don't. And we go for it.'

Kate thought about that for a moment. 'Are you saying Anais believes in love, and that that's pedestrian? Because I hate to break it to you, Scott, but I'm pedestrian in that way too. It's impossible *not* to believe in love in my family. They throw it at you in great gooey clumps, whether you want it or not.'

'Ah, but that's a different kind of love to the romantic stuff.'

'The principles are the same. Real love, of *any* kind, glories in a person's strengths and talents and…and their flaws too. *Especially* their flaws. It accepts and it…it heals. It lets you just…*be*. Be who you are. A lot of divorces happen because that's *not* the kind of love on offer.' Stop. Breath. 'And that's when the lawyers come in—earning thousands of dollars negotiating whether it's Mr or Mrs X who gets five hundred dollars' worth of groceries in the settlement. And that's a true story.'

'But it's not about the groceries, is it?'

'No. It's about power. Punishing someone because they can't love you enough, or don't need you enough, or won't give you enough.' She shivered. 'It makes you wonder…'

'Wonder?'

'Why you'd ever let someone have that power over you.'

'And that is why you and I—two sex-crazed cynics—are meant for each other.'

'For the grand total of two more weeks.'

'Rollover clause, remember?' He eyed her closely. 'You're not finished with me yet, are you, Kate?'

'No, I'm not finished with you.' She clinked her glass

against Scott's beer bottle. 'Here's to not having to get divorced. Not that Clearys get divorced any more than Knights.'

'But—' He broke off, shook his head. 'You said your mother's in favour of divorce.'

'And so she is—for all those people silly enough to get married in the first place.'

'You mean…? Hang on, I'm not getting this.'

'Clearys don't get divorced because they don't get married.'

'You mean like…ever?'

'Not in recent history.'

'Your mother?'

'Nope.'

'*Her* mother?'

'Absolutely not—Gran was all about free love.'

'Molly and Maeve's parents?'

'No. It's easier, you know, not to rely on a man. Or, in reverse, a woman. But don't misunderstand me—our fathers were in our lives as much as they wanted to be, and it worked very well.' She smiled. 'Gus—my father—and Aristotle—Shay and my other sister Lilith's father—even get along well together.'

'So it's one of those weird, blended, out-there families that are going to be the ruin of civilisation? The Knight family would be horrified!'

'Are *you*? Horrified?'

'I said the Knight family. I'm not really part of that.'

She looked at him sharply. 'What does that mean?'

He shrugged. 'I need another beer,' he said, and went into the apartment.

Kate followed him inside. Waited while he grabbed a beer from the fridge.

'What's your family like, Scott?'

'Doctors.'

'No—I mean, what are they *like*?'

'Well…doctors.' He hunched a shoulder. 'You've met

Hugo. He's pretty up and down perfect. That's the standard.
My family is *not* weird, blended and out-there. More like
stultifyingly conventional.'

'So you're…what? The black sheep?'

'More like the sheep with second-grade wool.'

'Okay, what does *that* mean?'

He took a pull of his beer. 'Nothing. Just that growing
up as a Knight is… Well, it's nothing a Cleary would understand.'

'Try me.'

He paused. Looked at her. Opened his mouth. Closed it.
Shook his head. 'Forget it, Kate.' One of those infuriating
smiles that meant nothing. 'It's not *germane*. And— Ah, the
intercom. Better go let your sister in.'

If Shay and Rick were surprised to find a man at Kate's
they didn't show it. And Scott—well, he was all smooth
charm. But in that closed-off, *keep your distance* way. A
way that made Shay, who was unusually perceptive, narrow her eyes at him.

As Shay and Rick went to get the girls there was silence.

Kate racked her brain for a way to break it—a way to
break through the sudden wall of reserve that was between
them.

But in the end Scott was the one to break the silence. 'So,
Kate, I owe you.' He reached in his pocket for his wallet.

'Wh—What?'

'Money for the pizza.' He handed over some notes.

Kate stared at the money in her hand as he returned his
wallet to his pocket. 'Scott…?'

'Fifty-fifty, remember?' he said with a meaningless smile.
'And now I'd better hit the ro—'

He broke off as Rick and Shay reappeared, carrying Maeve
and Molly, who were drowsy and tousled and lovable.

Kate kissed the girls. And then watched, fascinated, as
they each in turn leaned towards Scott for him to kiss them
too. She saw Scott blush as he did so. The cool reserve was

gone for those few moments, replaced by something peril-
ously close to tenderness.

Scott…and children.

Something he couldn't have because he never stayed with
a woman long enough? Or because he was a Knight. Or…
or what?

Shay, won over in that instant, smiled at him, and Scott
blushed again.

And then Kate and Scott were alone again, and she wondered what was going to happen next. Given the way he'd
kissed her out on the terrace, by rights she should have been
flat against the door with Scott all over her the moment it
closed behind her family…but Kate had a feeling that was
not going to happen.

Scott took her face between his hands and she waited,
breathless and curious.

'You're so beautiful, Kate,' he said, but that fact didn't
seem to make him happy.

He leaned close, put his forehead on hers and just stopped.
Not moving, not even breathing.

Kate wanted so badly to wrap her arms around him and
tell him everything would be all right, even though she didn't
know what was wrong. But she stayed exactly as she was.
Soaking in this moment where nothing happened, nothing
changed.

And then Scott released her, stepped back. Smiled one of
those smiles that didn't reach his eyes.

'I hope you appreciate that I did *not* kiss you then,' he said.
'Please note for future reference that I am capable of obeying
the rules. No kissing if it isn't going to lead to sex, right?'

'But I thought—'

'I just—I just think I'd better go home tonight.'

'But you can still go home tonight. I mean, after…'

But at the look on his face—closed-off, determined—
Kate forced herself to stop. She wasn't going to beg. Not any

man. Ever. And especially not this one, who was already running rings around her in every possible way.

Ring-running. For her own mental health, it was going to have to stop.

So she smiled, as remote as he was. 'Yeah, we're over our target, right?'

'Right,' Scott said. 'I'll see you tomorrow, then—new week, new target.'

'Not tomorrow,' Kate said.

'But you said Sunday.'

'And now I'm saying no.'

His eyes narrowed. 'That sounds like pique, Kate. And we don't have room for pique in our contract.'

'No, we don't have any allowances for pique in our contract, Scott,' she said, very cool. 'This is not pique. I wasn't expecting you tonight—as you know very well. I was, in fact, planning to do some work once I'd put the girls to bed. Now I have to play catch-up tomorrow. So thank you.'

'Ouch. I'm going to need that stapler,' Scott said.

Then with a mock salute he was gone.

Kate looked at the door, wondering exactly what had happened out there on the terrace.

She crossed her arms against a chill premonition that things between them were not going to work out the way either of them expected.

CHAPTER NINE

THE NEXT MORNING Scott was back at Rushcutters Bay, his finger frozen just short of the intercom buzzer, wondering what the hell he was doing.

Kate had made it clear she was going to be busy today, doing the work she'd planned to do the previous night if not for his inconvenient arrival. Code—and not exactly secret—for *I don't want to see you.*

And yet here he was, trying to work out how to charm his way into her apartment, how to apologise for the way he'd run away last night. The way he *kept* running away.

But how did you tell someone you'd run because you were in too deep and wanted to pull back—even as you were fronting up for more?

He hadn't intended to see her last night after she'd sent that irritatingly dismissive email about babysitting, but... well, he'd *wanted* to see her, dammit!

And he'd also known that if he *didn't* see her he'd be looking down the barrel of another sleepless night. Because his frazzled brain kept circling round and around everything that had happened on Thursday night, urging him to prove to himself that the way he'd been feeling was a one-off, all caught up in the unforeseen angst of the occasion—Hugo; that shared moment when they'd both just *got* it; his winning—*winning*! *That* was why he'd smiled at her—okay, he smiled a *lot*...he even smiled at *her* a lot...but not like that. And *that* explained the sex too—so straighty one-eighty that it should *not* have seared him like a barbecued steak, and yet it had been on fire, plated up, skip the garnish, *delicious.*

So, yeah, last night, he'd intended to prove the one-offness of it all to himself. To turn up off-schedule, joke about Valentine's Day, dazzle her with a little light-hearted banter, with the girls there to run interference and put the kybosh on anything emotional. Then they'd have sex in a manner in keeping with their contract—he'd thought of something highly technical that would mean they'd have to concentrate on not breaking a bone, so no time for losing themselves in the moment—and *voilà*: back to normal. Head back in the right place, heart untouched.

No watching her sleep or tracing his finger over her eyebrow, no sniffing her damned perfume when he was alone in her bathroom. None of that creepy stuff.

But instead his dumbass brain had started shooting off on tangents until he'd started thinking about kids. Redheaded, grey-eyed kids. How it would be to bring up kids the Cleary way, with people flinging gooey clumps of love at you—not the Knight way, where you had to prove yourself every damned day just to get a frosty nod. And then had come the blinding knowledge that he'd have to be married to the mother of his kids, so maybe the Cleary way would never work for him.

And then it had hit him that he was really, actually, contemplating fatherhood. *Fatherhood! Him!*

In too deep—caring too much—needing more—*run*.

He should have been happy to be barred today, so he could get his brain out of his gonads and back where it was supposed to be. But after one more sleepless night, thinking about that look on her face as he'd left, here he was.

Because… Well, what had that remote smile of hers meant? That she was finished with him? Well, no. Not happening until *he* was ready. So he was going to charm her into *not* finishing with him—while simultaneously stepping away from the too-deep chasm that was yawning at his feet.

Simple, right?

Yeah, simple. Sure.

Oh, for the love of God, man up!

He let his finger land on the buzzer. Waited, drumming his fingers on the wall.

By God, she'd better be at home after spinning him that line about work. She'd better not be out somewhere, with someone, doing something. Or he would— Would— Well, he'd…explode! Or…or something.

'Hello?' Her voice, husky and gorgeous—and for a moment his breath caught.

Get a grip. Get a damned grip!

'It's me,' he said, and winced—because that aggressive tone of voice was not charming.

Long pause. Followed by an arctic, 'Yes?'

'Can I come up?'

'Why?'

'Because I want to see you.'

'You saw me last night. That will have to tide you over until I can spare the time.'

Pause. Pages being riffled. What the hell—? Was she checking her schedule?

'Probably Tuesday.'

Yes, she'd been checking her schedule! Scott felt his temper start to simmer.

'No,' he said, and there was *absolutely* nothing charming about that snapped-out word.

'I beg your pardon?' Past arctic and heading towards ice age.

'Let me come up and explain.'

'The contract doesn't require explanation.'

The freaking *contract*. They didn't *need* a contract to have sex. He hadn't *asked* for a damned contract, had he? She'd *forced* it on him.

'All right, I won't explain,' he said through clenched teeth. He made a mammoth effort to rein in his slipping temper. Charm. Charm, charm, *charm*. 'So…since I'm obviously not coming up, why don't you come down and keep me company while I have a cup of coffee at the cafe across at the marina? Ten minutes and you can get back to work.'

Long, long moment. He heard the breath she sucked in. Waited for the breath out—waited, waited…

And then the breath whooshed out and she said, albeit grudgingly, 'All right.'

Not exactly effusive, but Scott closed his eyes in relief.

Five minutes later she was there, wearing a maxi-dress in sky-blue and a pair of flat silver sandals, her hair swinging in a ponytail. Delectable Sunday-morning fare.

His temper disappeared as if by magic just at the sight of her. He wanted to kiss her so badly he automatically leaned in—but Kate flinched backwards.

'No kissing, remember?' she said.

'Sorry, Kate,' he said, trying to look chastened but not quite managing it. He was just so happy to see her. God, what was happening to him?

They walked in silence to the cafe. Ordered coffee at the counter. A long black for him; a macchiato for Kate. Took their cups to one of the tables closest to the jetty.

'About last night…' Scott said, diving in.

Kate stirred sugar into her coffee. 'I thought you weren't going to explain.'

He ignored that. 'It just got a little…a little…heavy. Talking about children—'

'A subject *you* raised.'

'And about… Well, about all that stuff.' Shaky little laugh. 'Love.' Grimace. 'And…and stuff. I didn't sign up for deep and meaningful. Neither of us did. So I'm not sure how all that came spewing out.'

'It happens,' Kate said. 'It's normal.'

'No, it's not. Not for me. It's not what we—'

'Signed up for,' she cut in dryly. 'Got it. No need to labour the point. And no need to explain, remember?'

'Anyway, I thought we needed a breather—that's all,' he mumbled, and hurriedly picked up his coffee, took a sip, burned his tongue and refused to show it. Because people

in control didn't burn their tongues on coffee. And he was.
In control. Definitely.

'And yet here you are, the very next morning. That's a
breather, is it?'

'I just— I wanted to—'

'Explain. Yep. Got it.'

Kate looked at him—the epitome of inscrutability. She
drew in a breath. Seemed on the verge of speaking. But then
something behind him caught her attention and her eyes
widened.

'Isn't that…? Yes, surely…'

But it was a murmur directed at herself, not him.

She refocused on Scott. 'That's Brodie, isn't it? He really
is as gorgeous as his photo.'

CHAPTER TEN

BRODIE.

Gorgeous Brodie.

Instinctively Scott hated that combination of words coming out of Kate's mouth.

But then the reality of her words hit.

Brodie. Here.

They were about to come face to face. *If* he could make himself turn around.

But for that first moment he was robbed of the ability to breathe, let alone move, as eight years of feelings rushed at him.

That one hot moment. The sense of betrayal. The bitterness. Shame at what he'd done. Regret at what he'd lost. And...loneliness. A confusing, potent, noxious mix he just couldn't seem to control the way he'd since learned to control everything else.

Kate was watching him. Any minute now she'd ask him what was wrong. It was a wake-up call to get it together—because he did *not* want to be asked.

He took a breath, pushed the feelings away, forced himself to turn.

Recognition in a split second. Brodie's walk. Unmistakable. A loose-limbed, relaxed amble. He was as beach-blond as he'd always been. Tanned. Wearing sunglasses. Boat shoes, jeans, pale blue shirt with the sleeves casually rolled up to the elbows. And a tattoo—an anchor—on the underside of one forearm.

Scott remembered that tattoo. He'd been impressed by it. And a little bit jealous. Because Knights didn't get tattoos—and yet when he'd seen Brodie's he'd wanted to be the kind of guy who *did*. Not that he couldn't have had one—

then *or* now. But deep down he'd always known it wasn't his thing. It was the rebelliousness of a tattoo that had appealed to him, not the reality of ink in his skin. Everything about breezy, laidback Brodie had appealed to Scott—who was the exact opposite.

He knew the instant Brodie recognised him from the slight hitch in his stride. The sunglasses were whipped off, the eyes widened, a smile started...then stopped. Replaced by wariness. Then the sunglasses were shoved into the pocket of his shirt—Brodie was not the kind of guy to hide behind sunglasses or anything else—and Brodie walked on, heading straight for them. He stopped at their table.

'Scott,' he said.

'Brodie.'

Okay, it was all a bit ridiculous. *Scott. Brodie.* Kate would be coughing up her name in a minute. Maybe the barista would pop out and give them a *Dean.*

Scott laughed—couldn't seem to help it. And he had the satisfaction of seeing surprise replace the wariness. It felt good.

'Join us for coffee?' he asked.

'Sure,' Brodie said, recovering from the surprise, and snagged a spare seat from the next table.

Kate reached out a hand to shake. 'I'm Kate. A...' Tiny, tiny pause. 'A friend of Scott's.'

Brodie smiled as he took her hand, said nothing—but Kate blushed.

She flicked a glance at Scott, then back to Brodie. 'I'm a friend of Willa's too. And Amy's.'

'Ah, you're *that* Kate.'

'Oh, dear, you're not going to make a lawyer joke, are you?'

'Fresh out of lawyer jokes, sorry!'

'Well, isn't *that* a breath of fresh air?' she said with another of those flicking looks. At Scott, then Brodie.

Scott felt the sting. So he'd made one lawyer joke—just

once! That didn't put him ahead of Dirty Martini Barnaby in the woeful pick-up line competition, did it?

'I'll go and get the coffee,' Kate said. 'What'll it be, Brodie?'

'Black. Same as Scott.'

Nod. Smile. And she was off.

'Girlfriend?' Brodie asked, once Kate was out of earshot.

Scott crossed his arms over his chest. Shook his head. 'Nothing like that.'

Pause. A long one.

Okay—they were back to ridiculous.

Time to suck it up and move on.

'Are we going to get all girly and talk about things?'

Brodie winced. 'God, I hope not.'

'Right. Good. Great.'

Arms were uncrossed. His hand held out. Brodie took it. Shook.

'That's it?' Brodie asked.

'Well, let's see…' Scott frowned, looking as if he was thinking deeply. 'We were best friends. A girl who never loved me—a girl I didn't really love—fell for you. I punched you. You got an attack of nobility and took off. She stayed and was miserable.' He shrugged. 'I'd say between the three of us we royally screwed that up. It's sure felt screwed up for the past eight years, and I'm kind of over everything about it. So, yeah—that's it. From my perspective at least.'

'I've missed you, you know—you bastard.'

'Hey—we're not getting all girly, remember?'

Brodie laughed. 'That's why I added the "bastard".'

'Yeah, well, "bastard" doesn't make it any less girly.'

'Still an uptight control freak, then.'

'And you're still…what? King of the hair braids?'

'The sisters have outgrown the braids.' Brodie shuddered, but he was laughing too. 'Thank God.'

Slight pause. But not uncomfortable.

And then the question just came out of Scott's mouth, as though it was just…time. 'So, have you seen her?'

'No.'

'Do you want to?'

Long pause. 'Eight years,' Brodie said.

And somehow Scott understood the world in those two words. 'Okay, enough said. But just so you know—it wouldn't bother me. Not any more.'

Brodie jerked his head backwards towards the cafe counter. 'Because of Red?'

Brodie looked over Scott's shoulder, saw Kate coming towards them with a coffee-laden tray. That rolling walk. So damned sexy.

He blinked. Swallowed a sigh. Shook his head. 'That's just an…arrangement.'

Kate arrived, distributed the coffee. Sat down. 'So, how's the luxury yacht touring business?' she asked Brodie. 'In Queensland, right?'

'I should warn you,' Scott broke in. 'Kate's main goal in life is to steal a boat and sail off on an adventure—except she can't sail.' He smiled at Kate, expecting her to share the joke. But she merely looked steadily back at him.

Brodie was smiling at her too, and she *did* smile at him—and Scott found himself gritting his teeth. *A contract. Just a contract—and this is why.*

'Well, Kate, I'm down for a couple of weeks,' Brodie said. 'I'll take you sailing. Unless…?' He glanced at Scott. 'Are *you* going to teach her?'

Scott shook his head quickly. 'I sold my boat.' He looked at Kate; she was still smiling at Brodie. *Just a contract.* 'She's all yours.'

He caught—just—an infinitesimal flinch, the blink of hurt on Kate's face, and wanted to call the words back. But it was too late. Her smile went megawatt—straight at Brodie. And Scott wanted to claim that wide, gorgeous mouth of hers right there and then, in front of Brodie and everyone else in the vicinity. Screw the no-kissing rule.

'If you're still here next Saturday, Brodie, I'll take you up on that,' Kate said, and then she was tossing back her macchiato—and that *had* to burn her damned tongue. Not that you could tell from the next blinding smile she beamed at Brodie!

Brodie and Kate discussed timing, swapped numbers, while Scott sat there like a statue—ice on the outside, volcano on the inside.

And then Kate put some money on the table and Scott had to grit his teeth again. Because—come *on*!—couldn't he even buy her a damned cup of coffee?

The contract. Fifty-fifty. No, you can't buy her a damned coffee.

'Work calls,' she said, all cheery and unconcerned. 'Bye, guys. See you Saturday, Brodie.'

Gone.

Brodie looked at Scott, who had yet to take a sip from his fresh cup.

'Are you insane?' Brodie asked conversationally.

Scott laughed, and if it had a slight edge of insanity he wasn't going to acknowledge it. 'Tell me about your business,' he said instead.

When Kate got back to her apartment she was so furious—and disillusioned, and…and *hurt*, she couldn't think straight.

God, she hoped Scott hadn't seen the hurt.

Not that Scott, who didn't *get* hurt, would ever understand it. He'd just think she was *piqued*. The way he had last night just because she'd finally taken a stand and told him not to turn up today.

Well, that had sure worked!

And she really *must* be a pathetic nymphomaniac. Because she'd been so glad to see him when she should have been annoyed. So very glad…right up until he'd told her he hadn't *signed up* for deep and meaningful.

Nobody signed up for deep and meaningful. It just…*happened.*

But not, apparently, to Scott.

Well, what had she expected? That two weeks of rock-your-hormones sex would somehow make her special? That the guy she was sleeping with might want to teach her to sail rather than palming her off on someone else? That he might actually introduce her to his friends so she didn't have to introduce herself, when she didn't have the remotest idea how to categorise their relationship for public consumption? That he might, somehow, claim her as someone just a little bit special?

The way she wanted to—

Ooohhhh.

She shuddered out a breath as reality hit her like a truck. She wanted to claim him. *Mine, mine, mine.*

Great! Just freaking great. Because Scott had made it pretty clear this morning that he was reading from a different script—and it wasn't a romance. To Scott she was a collection of body parts, transferable to his friend for any non-bedroom stuff!

She's all yours!

Well, *quid pro quo. There* was a legal term for Scott to mull over.

If she was nothing but a collection of body parts to him then he would be nothing but a collection of body parts to *her.*

Scott Knight: Kate Cleary's stud.

No more kissing. No dates that weren't really dates. No unscheduled drop-ins. No fireside chats. Nothing except sex. Only twice a week, because she was no longer in a negotiating mood. Starting with a Play Time that would fry his nether regions!

Before she could think twice she grabbed her phone, pulled up Scott's number and got texting.

Play Time. Tuesday. 9 p.m. Ellington Lane.

That would shock him. He'd be sitting there with Brodie, never dreaming she'd text him so soon after that dismal coffee catch-up. He probably expected her to be lying face-down on her bed, crying into her pillow because she was *piqued*. Well, he could just—

Ding.

Text message. She grabbed her phone. Opened Scott's text message.

Roger that.

With a smiley face.

A…a *smiley face*?

Now, you see—that was why he wasn't the right man for her.

Or maybe why he is.

'Yes, thank you, subconscious. Not helpful.'

Scott was champing at the bit as he approached Ellington Lane on Tuesday night.

He had no idea what fantasy Kate had dreamt up to carry out in this dingy, narrow, deserted laneway, but hopefully it didn't involve his murder—because Ellington Lane certainly looked as if it regularly saw a dead body, and Kate surely must want to kill him after Sunday.

He wasn't even certain she was going to turn up, given she hadn't bothered answering any of his thousand calls since then.

But he was here waiting anyway—he who *never* had sex in public places—so hungry for her he'd do anything.

He was going to make tonight *so* damned good for her. Use his body to show her he didn't mean what he'd said—because clearly he couldn't trust his malfunctioning brain to choose the right words.

He still couldn't believe he'd said it. *She's all yours.* Just because she'd smiled at Brodie and he'd wanted to grab her and demand she stop. Because she was his, his, *his*, and she was supposed to smile at *him*—got it?

God, he was a moron! *You're mine—so go with that guy instead, why don't you?*

He *deserved* to be standing here, lust-starved and desperate, in an ill-lit, deserted alley, wondering if she'd turn up, shivering at the thought of what she'd do to him, and just… well, *longing* for her.

He took a deep breath, trying to steady himself.

And suddenly there she was.

CHAPTER ELEVEN

SCOTT'S HEART LURCHED as Kate took one step. Stopped.

She was backlit by a street lamp just outside the lane. Standing with her legs slightly apart, looking tough. Tight pants, high boots, hands on hips, wearing some kind of cap.

She started walking towards him—very slowly, very deliberately. Halfway, he could see she was wearing a police uniform—but a sexed-up, skintight version.

His mouth went dry—so dry that when she asked, 'What seems to be the problem?' he couldn't answer.

And then she was in front of him, and he could smell tuberose, and he wanted to throw himself at her feet and beg.

'Not talking?' she asked, and there was a snap in her voice. 'Then I'd say you're up to no good. Turn around, hands wide on the wall.'

He did as he was told.

She kicked between his feet. 'Spread 'em.'

He *spread 'em* with alacrity, and then breathed out a long, silent sigh of surrender as she plastered herself against his back.

'So… Are you behaving yourself?' she asked, and chuckled, low and breathy, right in his ear.

'Yes, Officer,' he said—or at least he tried to, but it came out as a half-strangled gargle.

'Now, why don't I believe you? What's in your pockets?'

'Nothing.'

'I think I'll check for myself.'

Next moment her hands were diving into the back pockets of his jeans.

'Condom,' she said. 'Not exactly "nothing". Not soliciting, are you?'

'No.'

'No *what*?'

'No, Officer.'

'I'll hold on to this,' she said, and he imagined her sliding the condom into the back pocket of her tight, tight pants.

'Right. Let's check your other pockets,' she said.

And her hands were *there*, digging into his front pockets, making his heartbeat go off like a cracker as she 'accidentally' nudged against the erection straining fiercely against the denim.

'All clear,' she breathed against his ear. 'So—why don't you just tell me what you've been up to so I don't have to keep searching?'

'But I've done nothing wrong, Officer.'

'So let me ask you, buddy: do you know the meaning of the term *ignorantia juris non excusat*?'

Oh, God. God, God, God.

'No. But it sounds…sexy.'

'Well, it's not sexy,' she said, despite the fact that she was unbuttoning his jeans, sliding his zipper down, sliding her hands inside, over his erection, squeezing, stroking. 'It means ignorance of the law is not an excuse.'

He groaned.

'Am I hurting you?' she asked.

'No. No, Officer, you're not hurting me.'

'Then why are you groaning?'

'Can't…*ahh*…help it. Sorry. J-Just what law am I ignorant of?'

'The law that says you're not allowed to bribe a police officer.'

'But I'm not,' he said, just as her hands went beneath his underwear, cool and silky and freaking *wonderful*. Another groan slipped out. Could a man die of lust? Because he was on the way.

'Then maybe you should *think* about bribing me, so I'll let you off the hook.'

'Um… Um… Um…' Seriously, his brain was fricasseed.

'Something that doesn't involve a condom, since I've confiscated that,' she said.

'Um…'

'Turn around.'

He turned fast enough to give himself a corkscrew knee injury. Reached automatically for her.

'No touching an officer,' she barked. 'Just stand there. Stand there and take it like a man.'

Before he knew what was happening she'd shoved him against the wall. And then she was on her knees in front of him, dragging his jeans down, just low enough to free him. Holding the base of him with one hand, cupping his balls with the other, she licked the very tip of him. Delicate, fluttery…gradually moving down the shaft, back up, down, then up. Alternately kissing and licking. Gradually increasing the pressure of her tongue, her lips.

He wanted to touch her hair, but she'd wound it up under the police cap. And looking at that cap as she worked on him was getting him more excited than he'd ever been in his life.

She tilted her head back, replaced her mouth with her hands, looked up at him, parted her lips, licked that heavy top lip…and with a quick, wicked smile closed her mouth over him.

Scott let loose with a whole string of groaning cries as she sucked him, using her lips, her tongue, her teeth, even the roof of her mouth. Stretching him, laving him, devouring him. Her hands were moving everywhere her mouth wasn't until he was half insane with need. He felt the orgasm building, clawing to get out.

And then she did something with her tongue, and he looked down at the police cap, caught a glimpse of pale skin as she angled her head and her mouth performed a twist he'd never experienced before, and it was rushing at him.

'Kate! Kate, I'm going to come!' he said in urgent warning.

But she just kept right on going, shifting so that her hands were gripping his hips, keeping him inside her mouth, and he thought for a moment he was going to pass out with the pleasure of it. She kept up the pressure right through his explosion of a release, as his hips jerked under her hands and he spilled himself to the point of exhaustion.

And then she got to her feet. Looked at him as she licked that top lip again. 'So, whatever you were doing tonight before I caught you—' as though she'd just written him a ticket '—don't do it again.'

And then she turned, started walking away.

Scott couldn't believe, at first, that she would just leave him like that—but she kept going.

'Kate!' he called out, pulling up his jeans.

Stop. Turn. 'It's Officer Cleary.'

'I'll come with you. I owe you.'

'Is that another bribe?' She shook her head. 'Now, you see, that's why I don't associate with criminals.'

'But—'

'You'll receive a message from the station in a few days, once I've cleared your name, and then we'll see.'

She turned again, walked briskly down the lane. And was gone.

He finished tucking in his shirt. Feeling both incredibly sated and hugely unsatisfied.

Because she was gone. Without having let him touch her once.

Gone. Just like Sunday morning.

Gone.

One thing Scott knew was that he wasn't a fan of this 'gone girl' thing. He was going to have to let her know he didn't appreciate her just leaving. Like, *bang*, leaving.

Even if it *was* essentially what he'd done to her on Saturday night—and without giving her any kind of release at all. But he'd had a *reason*. Self-preservation! Her? Tonight? What possible reason could she have had?

Bang. Gone.

Nope. He didn't like it one bit.

The next day Scott left two phone messages for Kate.

Her response was to text him back.

Play Time. Thursday. Your house. 7 p.m.

He swore long and loud. Play Time was all very well, but he wanted to talk to her. That interrupted conversation from Sunday morning was still heavy on his mind and he wanted to fix it. Because things didn't feel...*right*.

He tried to call her again—she didn't pick up. So he called her office, spoke to Deb. Received the message that Kate was interstate, working on a child custody case.

'And it's a messy one,' Deb told him. 'So you've got no chance of getting hold of her and please don't try. She's...'

He could feel the hesitation. Teetering, teetering... *Go on, tell me, tell me.* But no.

'Look, just leave her to it,' Deb said, and hung up.

He found himself hanging on to the phone, reluctant to let it go. As if it was some line of communication he didn't want to snap.

Which was just plain stupid.

He forced himself to disconnect.

He worried about what Deb had said. *'She's...'* Just the one word. Hesitant, hanging, worrying.

She's...what? She's...not interested in you any more? She's...having a meltdown? Having a biopsy? Eating chicken for lunch. What, dammit? *What?*

He paced around his office, needing to speak to her, knowing he couldn't.

Focusing on the first thing that had popped into his head—that she wasn't interested in him any more—calmed him a little. Because if that were true she wouldn't have sent him that Play Time text.

And they had a *contract*—which might be stupid but at least meant that even if she was over him she still had to see him for another week and a half. So he had time to work on her, get her back onside. Time to make the sex so phenomenal she'd be sorry she didn't have a clause demanding seven nights a week instead of a lousy two.

Starting Thursday, when he saw her again. At *his* house, this time. In *his* bed.

He never brought women home, because...well, *because*. But Kate...?

He sucked in a breath as the image of her in his house shimmered in his head.

Would she like it?

In his bed?

How would she look there?

Not that those thoughts were *germane*! The *germane* thing was that it would be the perfect opportunity to gauge whether the wattage of their sexual attraction needed to be amped up. Although, frankly, much more wattage might just finish him off.

A new image popped into his head. Kate on her knees in that dark alley, going down on him. Refusing to allow him to touch her. Just leaving him there.

Okay, so he *hadn't* calmed down.

He wouldn't be calm until he spoke to her. Until he knew what was going on with her.

He wouldn't be calm until *she* was calm.

Because he knew, *knew*, she wasn't calm. He'd heard the worry in Deb's voice. A child custody case. The kind that hit Kate the hardest. She would be stressed. And...and *grieving*. Interstate—on her own. With nobody to hold her and tell her it was going to be all right, even if it wasn't. Just to *be* there. With her—for her.

And then he stopped himself. She had a family to turn to. A large, loving family. She didn't need him.

Sex. No strings. That was what they had. She'd made that plain by responding to his voicemail messages with a text. She was going through hell…but for him she offered Play Time. Because that was the deal. He'd teased her that she was falling behind on the fantasies, so she was dishing them up. Twice in one week. Any man would want that. Phillip the aged barrister would be *thrilled* with that.

Scott found that his hands had balled into fists and determinedly unclenched them. Flexed them. Took a deep, calming breath.

Better.

It was no good getting bent out of shape over Phillip. Over Play Time. Or over Kate being alone dealing with hell. No damned good.

So he would take Deb's advice. He would wait until Thursday. He would see what fantasy she came up with. He would respond sexually.

And that would be all.

CHAPTER TWELVE

KATE TOOK EXTRA-SPECIAL care getting ready for Play Time on Thursday. Her hair was swinging loose, artfully dishevelled, and she had on her favourite red lipstick—which was fine for today because there would be no kissing.

She was wearing her sexiest underwear. Nude mesh and lace, complete with suspender belt—and she'd gone for ultra-sheer black stockings as a contrast. Achingly high black stilettos. A taupe trench coat, tied but not buttoned.

That was it. Not one thing more. Perfect for the role she was playing.

A role that would not involve any of those pesky *deep and meaningful* fireside chats.

Scott would be happy about that. And, frankly, she was happy about it too. Having spent two soul-destroying days fighting to get her client's little boy back, 'Kate Cleary' deserved the night off. Tomorrow she would take up the legal cudgels again—but tonight, Kate wanted to be someone else.

When Kate arrived at Scott's house in East Sydney she had to recheck his business card to make sure she had the right address—because she was standing in front of an old church. She'd already guessed Scott's house was going to be special, if Silverston was anything to go by. But this was something else. She couldn't wait to see inside.

No! She caught herself up. She wasn't a starry-eyed girlfriend, about to get a guided tour of her boyfriend's architectural wonder of a home. Scott—who hadn't even invited her here—was probably in there pacing the floor, hating the idea of her invading his private space. So she wouldn't give him the satisfaction of being interested.

She noted the intercom in place of a doorbell, which reminded her that his house doubled as a second office. Perfect, since she was here on 'business'.

She waited outside for seven o'clock to hit, using the time to layer on the persona she'd chosen, mentally steeling herself to resist the first heart-melting look at him, the first touch. And then, on the dot, she pushed the button.

Instant answer.

'Kate?' Sounding anxious. 'There in two seconds.'

'Oh, Mr Knight, has there been a mistake?' she asked, all breathy and flustered.

Pause. And then, 'Kate? It *is* Kate, right?'

'It's *Lorelei*, Mr Knight. Don't you remember? You booked a home visit. Are you going to buzz me in?'

Another pause. Longer.

He would be processing that. Kate's voice giving a name he'd never heard, referring to a job he hadn't booked.

And then the intercom clicked off. So…was he *not* going to buzz her in?

But less than ten seconds later the door opened and he was there. He took her arm, drew her in. Tried to kiss her.

'Oh, sorry, Mr Knight. Miss Kitty doesn't like her girls to kiss the clients.'

His jaw tightened, but he said nothing.

Despite Kate's best efforts she couldn't help giving the space just one sweeping glance. Soaring arched ceilings, like a…well, like a *church*. Stained-glass windows, stark white walls, honey wood floors, a staircase that provided a pop of colour, with steps painted a vivid red, leading up to a mezzanine.

Enough! Stop!

'Where do you want me, Mr Knight?' she asked.

He gestured to the staircase. 'Go up.'

She walked quickly to the stairs and ascended. She paused at the top, needing direction—and had to close her eyes to stop herself peering over the half-wall. She was not going to look again. Not, not, *not*.

'There,' Scott said from behind her—and she opened her eyes to find him pointing to a long, intricately carved wooden screen at one end of the mezzanine floor.

Her heart started to race as she approached the screen. She was so excited to see what was behind it. And when she stepped around it she gasped. Just couldn't keep it in.

More stained-glass windows—taking the place of a fancy bedhead—dominated the space. The walls were painted a dull gold. A huge bed of dark wood with a blood-red coverlet sat on a raised stone dais. There were Persian rugs on the wood floor surrounding the dais. Antique chairs—grand and austere—were positioned either side of the stone slab, with candlesticks as tall as Scott beside them. The room was heartbreakingly, unexpectedly beautiful.

Kate schooled her features to show nothing as she turned back to Scott and smiled—a professionally vacant smile.

He was watching her with a hint of disapproval that she forced herself to ignore. Conservative Scott Knight *would* disapprove of a prostitute—but that didn't mean he wouldn't enjoy the experience.

She undid her belt, held the coat wide. 'Do you like what you see, Mr Knight?'

He swallowed, hard, as his eyes slid down her body and stuck at the tops of her black stockings. 'Yes,' he said. 'I want to touch you.'

'You can touch. Just no kissing.' And with that, she shrugged out of the coat and went to lay it on one of the chairs.

But she didn't make it that far. Because Scott was after her in a heartbeat.

Kate shivered as he grabbed her, as he spun her to face him, as he yanked her hair back to give him access to her neck, as he licked the pulse beating there.

And then he lowered his head, going straight for her nipple, taking it into his mouth through the mesh of her bra, sucking hard, harder, until she cried out. He didn't stop, just moved to the other nipple, then back again. Back and forth.

She was a quivering mess of nerves and need by the time he stepped back, took her coat and threw it at the chair.

He swallowed hard again as his eyes dipped to her breasts. Her nipples were dark and distended, the mesh covering them wet. His hands moved to her breasts, fingers pinching where his mouth had been. Pinching, rolling. And then he was digging into the thin cups, tearing them down so that her nipples popped over the tops, and his mouth was back, suckling and nipping and licking her.

Her hands were in his hair, pulling hard enough to hurt— but to keep him there, not to drag him away. She could feel the unbearable wetness between her thighs, wanted his hands there, his mouth.

As though he'd divined that, he dropped to his knees, kissed the tops of her stockings—one, then the other—and licked, *slooowly*, along the top of each, where her thighs were naked. Kate was scared she'd collapse on the spot, it was so erotic.

And then, completely at odds with the languor of that, he yanked her panties down to her knees and shoved his tongue between her legs. Her tangled underwear trapped her and limited Scott's access, forcing him to concentrate his tongue in one ravaging line. *So...damned...good.* She heard his ragged breathing, felt his fingers digging into the backs of her thighs, hard enough to bruise.

He growled something, impatient, and next moment was dragging her down onto the rug, ripping at her underwear, manoeuvring her onto her hands and knees. And then he was behind her, his mouth on her again, sucking her, forcing his tongue inside her until she was panting and whimpering with need.

A quick rustling sound, but his mouth didn't stop. Condom. She heard the packet tear. Zip opening. She imagined him sheathing himself. Knew he would be inside her soon.

She pushed herself back against his mouth, urging him wordlessly to hurry, to fill her.

He moved, covered her, his mouth at her ear. 'You're going to have to ask me,' he breathed.

'Please…*please*.'

'Please what?'

'I want you inside me. Do it. Inside—*now*.'

The words weren't even out of her mouth before he'd shoved himself into her. Holding her hips, screwing into her as though he had to get close, closer, closer still. Up to the hilt. Over and over. Pounding, pounding, pounding. And then he tensed, coming with a loud cry. His hands reached for her waist, yanked her upright, her back against his chest, and he was feeling for her clitoris, fingers forking either side, perfect pressure.

Ah, ahh, ahhhh.

'Come for me, Kate. Come now…come.'

And, in a blast of almost excruciating pleasure, she exploded into orgasm.

Slowly, Scott withdrew from her. Sat back, turned her, hoisting her onto his lap

He tried again to kiss her, and she drew back. 'No kissing,' she said, but was horrified to find her voice wobbling.

Even worse—he'd heard it too.

He looked at her—sharp, concerned. 'What is it, Kate?'

'Lorelei. And no kissing.'

'I'm not kissing Lorelei. I'm kissing Kate,' Scott said.

He coaxed her to open her mouth, took his leisurely time, letting his tongue move from licking her lips to sliding inside.

After a long, delicious moment he stopped, edged a fraction away, smiled into her eyes. That smile she'd only seen once—that night—but it was even more devastating now, because it was layered with gentleness.

I am in such trouble here.

'Kate…' he said, and his voice shook.

Such trouble. And she didn't need trouble.

Steeling herself, she smiled back. 'Lorelei,' she corrected. 'And that will be two thousand dollars, Mr Knight.'

The shock on Scott's face had her shrinking inside, but she forced herself to hold his eyes.

And then he smiled again—but it was back to the jukebox, pick a smile and whirl. 'Your prices are too low. I would have paid five. In fact, I *will* pay five. Because, as I recall, I booked Lorelei's services for a full night.'

'We don't stay overnight, Scott…you and I.' *Uh-oh*, the wobble.

'Miss Kitty says Lorelei *does*. And if you want your five thousand dollars that's what you're going to have to do.' He gave her a boost off his lap. 'So up you go. Whatever you've still got on, get it off. Then get into that bed.'

The next morning, after *Lorelei* had belted herself into her trench coat and left, Scott threw down three cups of coffee. He needed the caffeine to get his brain and his body functioning again.

But it didn't work.

Something was bothering him. Very deeply.

And it was… Well, it was Play Time.

The whole 'Lorelei' thing was eating at him. After that one frenzied bout of lovemaking on the rug, when he'd kissed Kate, he'd felt such an overwhelming burst of joy. Kate…in his arms, in his house, and he'd wanted her so damned much.

And she'd responded by asking him for her fee.

So he'd decided to get his money's worth. All night long he'd been at her, taking her with lips, tongue, fingers, his never-ending hard-on. And she'd met him move for move, always receptive—as 'Miss Kitty' expected—never saying no, opening her arms, her legs.

Everything but her mouth.

Because he'd tried to kiss her many times, and each time she'd pulled away with a coyly admonishing slap on the wrist, the shoulder, the butt, and a reminder of Miss Kitty's rules.

He'd tried to talk to her in those respite periods while they'd recharged their burnt-out batteries. About the child custody case. Her mother's art. Maeve and Molly, Shay and Lilith, Gus and Aristotle. Even about Deb. But every time he'd been frozen into crunchable cubes by her vacant 'Lorelei' stare.

The end result was that although he could have written his own sex manual after experimenting so comprehensively with Kate's body during the night, he wasn't satisfied.

And the flat fact was he didn't *like* Play Time.

There. He'd admitted it.

He must be certifiable, but he couldn't seem to whip up enthusiasm for any more fantasy-land stuff. It was like the sexual version of Brodie's tattoo—nice in theory, but just not him. He must be more of a Knight than he'd thought. Conservative. Boring, even.

Did Kate find him boring? In bed? Out of it? Both? Because she was suddenly very interested in Play Time. No kissing. No talking. Just role play. Was Play Time the nonnautical equivalent of a yacht heading to the Whitsundays? Taking Kate away from humdrum in the bedroom?

He put his coffee cup down with a clatter.

She'd made him *pay* for it! He almost hadn't believed it when Kate had demanded his cheque for five thousand dollars—and then had actually taken it when he'd jokingly written it out, before breezing out of the house.

A house she hadn't expressed the slightest interest in.

And his house was worth *some* level of interest from the woman he was exclusively sleeping with, dammit.

Not good enough, Kate.

He wanted to know what she thought about it. And he was going to force her to tell him. Did she like it? Hate it? Want to change it? *What?*

Scott gave her three hours—time to slough off that annoying Lorelei—then called her mobile. No answer. So he called her office.

Deb picked up the phone—and told him in no uncertain terms he wouldn't be getting a look-in that day because Kate was in back-to-back meetings.

Well, he wasn't going to put himself through the embarrassment of having his call go to voicemail, as had been happening with monotonous regularity. He would email her instead. And if she didn't respond he would… He would… He would do something as yet undetermined! But *something*, at any rate.

Calmly, rationally, unemotionally, he tapped out a message suggesting they catch up for dinner that night and fired it off, knowing she'd pick up the email on her smartphone whether she was in a meeting or not.

And then he waited, refreshing his emails every thirty seconds, working himself into a lather over the fifty-fifty rule she'd probably insist on when the bill came tonight. Well, screw her stupid fifty-fifty rule—*he* would be picking up the tab. Like a normal guy who *wasn't* a complete arsehole would do when he took a woman out for dinner.

Refresh, refresh, refresh…
Come on—respond!
Fifteen minutes later his phone buzzed.
Text message.
His stomach clenched as he reached for his phone. Because he just knew.
And, yep, there it was.

Play Time. Sunday. Noon. My apartment.

Scott hurled the phone across the room.

CHAPTER THIRTEEN

KATE SAW THE Whitsundays girls in their usual corner table at Fox on Friday night, cocktails already in hand, and thought, *Thank heaven*. A rowdy, uncomplicated girls' night out was exactly what she needed.

Jessica, who was facing the entrance, was the first to notice her across the crowded floor of the bar area, and she waved enthusiastically as Kate squeezed her way across the floor.

Willa slid a Manhattan—Kate's favourite cocktail—to her as she collapsed into her seat.

Kate, surprised and touched by Willa's prescience, kissed her.

'I knew you'd need it.' Willa's smile was full of sympathy. 'How did the case end up?'

Kate eased the elastic from her hair and ran a tired hand through the strands. 'Victory for Team Cleary.'

'Fantastic!'

'But it was harrowing, even for a jaded cynic of a lawyer.'

'You're not a jaded cynic,' Willa said. 'Or you wouldn't care so deeply.'

Kate felt a little prickle of tears—and that just underscored how wrung-out she was, because she never let her emotions show in public. She blinked the tears away, smiling determinedly.

'Whatever I am, I sure need this!' she said, picking up her glass and half draining it. 'And now—a *fun* topic of conversation, please.'

Amy laughed. 'Well, you're just in time to hear Willa tell us about her most romantic moment with Rob. Will that do?'

'That will do very, very nicely!' Kate said. 'But first…' She drained the rest of her Manhattan and signalled to a passing server for another round of drinks for all four of them. 'Better! Okay, Willa darling, spill it!'

'I'm not sure you guys will think it's romantic, but…oh, God, it *is*!'

'Don't make us beg!' Amy said.

'Well…Rob recommended me to a chief financial officer…'

'And…?' Amy urged.

'For a vitamin distribution company.'

'And…?' Jessica prompted.

Willa sucked her mojito through a straw. 'Rob told him I was super-bright!'

'And so you are, my darling,' Kate said.

'And…and brilliant!'

'Nice,' Jessica added.

'And that I knew about foreign-owned entities, so maybe I could help find a creative solution to a problem the company was having.'

Kate laughed. 'Okaaaay… That's not exactly floating my boat just yet, but I'm hoping something juicy is coming up.'

Willa beamed around at them, glowing with love. 'The CFO said they'd had a dozen accountants try to find a solution and fail. He said Rob had assured him I would be able to help. And I *did*! And I got *paid*!' She sighed, all satisfaction, and sucked up another mouthful of mojito. 'Isn't that romantic?'

Kate, Amy and Jessica stared at her, and then Amy burst out laughing.

One by one the others started laughing too.

'Hey, it's not funny,' Willa protested, but she had a smile lurking too.

Jessica said, 'Well, it's not exactly rose petals strewn over the bedcovers.'

Amy looked at Jessica. 'Seriously? *That's* your romantic fantasy? I would never have picked it, Miss I-can-play-basketball-and-change-a-car-tyre-when-the-game's-over.'

'Well, I *can* change a car tyre,' Jessica said. 'But I'd like a rose-petal-strewn-bed for afterwards. With candlelight. And being hand-fed ripe strawberries in the midst of it all. Lovely.' She raised her eyebrows at Amy. 'Why? What's yours, Miss Personality-plus?'

'Easy. A defender,' Amy said definitely. 'Someone who will ride in like a medieval knight on a destrier, catch me up and save me from…from…' She stopped, smiled a little sheepishly. 'Well, from danger,' she finished, then sighed. '*That's* romance.'

All three looked expectantly at Kate.

'Oh, no,' she said.

'Come on,' Amy begged.

Jessica sniggered. 'I'll bet it has something to do with Big Burt the handy vibrator.'

Kate felt herself blush—and then blushed harder when three jaws dropped simultaneously as the girls took in her colour change.

'No way!' Amy said.

'Not…not exactly,' Kate said, and then she threw in the metaphorical towel. 'Okay, you asked for it. It *does* happen to involve Burt. Not *Big* Burt, but his namesake. Burt *Lancaster*. And Deborah Kerr. And, no, Jessica, that does *not* mean I want to be in a three-way with Burt and Deborah, who are, in fact, both deceased. And, no, I never wanted to have sex with Burt Lancaster when he was alive either.'

'So what *does* it mean?'

'It means— Oh, dear, this is kind of embarrassing! Okay, it's all about my obsession with *From Here to Eternity*, which I really need to outgrow. And you have *got* to watch that movie, Jessica! It should be mandatory viewing for all women.'

'Okay—it's on the download list!' Jessica said promptly.

Kate ran a finger around the rim of her empty glass. 'When you get to the scene at the beach their passion is just so…so *strong*… And there's nothing they can do about it except acknowledge it and know that it's going to happen. They've been swimming, and they're at the shore, and she's lying on the sand, and then he's there with her, and she's in his arms. And he's kissing her like he can't help himself, with the waves breaking over them… And when she runs for drier ground he follows her, and drops to his knees, and basically…basically *falls* on her—like he's so damned hungry for everything about her… Well, *whew*!' She waved a hand in front of her heated face. 'That is *some* scene.'

Jessica was, likewise, fanning herself. 'It beats Willa's chief financial officer and my rose petals, that's for sure. And it gives Amy's destrier a nudge too.'

Kate laughed. 'Well, suffice to say if a man kisses me like that in the surf I'm his. From here to eternity.'

There was a moment of respectful silence.

And then Willa smiled. 'There's one thing I need to add to my own account,' she said, all smug. 'When Rob spoke to that vitamin-company CFO he said…' Pause. Blink. 'He said…' She paused again, went all dreamy-eyed. 'He said he'd trust me with his life.'

'Oh…' said Amy.

'Oh…' said Jessica.

'Oh,' said Kate. Deep breath. 'In that case, you win.'

Willa was glowing. 'Yes, I do, don't I?' she asked, delighted.

'I wonder what Chantal would say?' Amy mused. 'About *her* most romantic moment, I mean.'

Willa pondered that, eyes half closed. 'It would be something to do with dancing. The romance of swaying against a man, having him hold you close, showing you just by the way he looked at you that you were his…'

Four sighs as their fresh round of drinks was deposited—and then four dreamy sips.

'So Chantal's in your camp, Willa. She's already had her moment,' Amy said. 'With Brodie, I mean, at Weeping Reef.

Because that's what happened, right? The dance, the look that everyone could see?'

'It *was* sizzling,' Willa said.

Amy drained her glass. 'No wonder poor Scott got bent out of shape.'

Kate felt the blood drain from her face. What? *What?* 'Scott?' she said, and thanked all the saints in heaven that her voice had come out halfway normal.

'Oh, yeah—you don't know the story,' Willa said, sounding sad. 'Scott and Chantal were an item at Weeping Reef. *The* item. Until Brodie came on the scene. Actually, they were an item even after Brodie arrived. Chantal and Brodie didn't seem to like each other—except that they *did*, if you know what I mean, and just didn't recognise it. I think I was the only one who saw what was happening. Scott certainly didn't, and he was blindsided. Chantal was dancing with Brodie—which was no big deal. She loves dancing. Lives for it. But she could never get Scott onto the dance floor, and he never had a problem with her dancing with other men. But that night it was…*more*. Like a…a flash. The way they moved together…the way they looked at each other. Everyone knew in that one moment that Chantal and Brodie belonged together.'

Kate remembered asking Scott to dance at that dinner. Him telling her he didn't. Ever. Remembered him insisting on absolute fidelity in their contract.

'So what happened?' she asked through her aching throat.

'A huge argument—which ended with Scott slugging Brodie. Brodie took off, leaving Scott and Chantal at the resort together…but *not* together. Not *at all* together. Looking back, it all seems so needlessly dramatic, given nothing actually happened between Chantal and Brodie. But Scott and Brodie haven't spoken since.'

Uh-oh. Awkward. 'Actually, they…they *have* spoken,' Kate said, and took a quick silent breath to steady her nerves for the inquisition.

The three girls stared at her, waiting.

Kate took a slow sip of her Manhattan. 'I was having coffee with Scott, at the marina across the road from my place, on Sunday morning. And Brodie walked past. His boat's moored there.'

'Oh, my God!' Amy squealed. 'I don't know what part to ask about first. Coffee with Scott? How did *that* come about?'

'We've seen each other a couple of times since Willa's party.'

There was a long pregnant pause.

'It's nothing,' Kate said.

More silence.

'Really nothing,' she insisted. 'There was an…an attraction there, and we wanted to see if there was anything worth exploring. That's all.'

'And is there?' Jessica asked.

Kate took another sip. 'No. There really isn't,' she said, and felt the truth of that, the pang of it, pierce right through her heart. It took her a moment to recover from that certainty, to find her voice again. 'Anyway, Sunday morning he was in the area, so—'

Amy choked on her drink. '*In the area?* Are you *sure* there's nothing worth exploring?'

'Yes, in the area, and, no, there's nothing worth exploring,' Kate insisted, but she could feel the heat slash across her cheekbones. 'He buzzed my apartment and I went down to meet him.'

Very important to get the message out that he hadn't stayed the night at her place. She was a little embarrassed about hiding what was a straightforward arrangement from her friends, but she couldn't seem to up and confess. And it wasn't only the confidentiality clause stopping her. It just felt too…*painful*, somehow, to share.

'And what happened?' Amy asked.

'While we were sitting there drinking our coffee along came Brodie.'

'And then…? Come on, Kate,' Amy urged. 'The suspense is killing me.'

'All right. I'm just trying to remember it.' *As if she didn't!* 'There was some…tension. Yes, now that I think back there was definitely tension between them to start with. But I left them talking while I went to order, and by the time I returned, it was all quite amicable between them.'

'Thank God,' Willa said. 'They were so close, back in the day. Closer than brothers. It hasn't felt right, their estrangement.'

'So what happened next?' Amy asked. 'Is Brodie still here? I'd love to see him. And did they talk about Chantal?'

Chantal. The name whipped through Kate's bloodstream, breath-stealing.

Jealous. She was jealous—of something that had happened *eight years ago.* Because one woman had sneaked past Scott's defences, where *she* couldn't go. Where she was resolutely *blocked* from going. She picked up her glass to take another sip of her cocktail, realised it was empty but had no recollection of drinking it. Too much, too fast.

'I don't know what happened then because I left them to it,' she said. 'I knew they hadn't seen each other in a while, and I…I had work to finish. I haven't spoken to Scott since.'

Which wasn't strictly correct…but was still true. Officer Cleary and Lorelei had spoken to Scott—not Kate.

'Nobody was throwing punches, if that's any comfort to you,' Kate added. 'And one thing I *do* know is that Brodie is still in Sydney, because he's giving me a sailing lesson tomorrow.'

'Oh! You are *so* lucky!' Jessica said. 'I'd love to learn to sail.'

'Well, it's only one lesson,' Kate said. 'All I can really expect is to find out if I've got what it takes or if it will be like the time I tried Tai Chi—nice idea, but not going to happen. Why don't you come too, Jessica?'

Jessica sighed. 'Nah—I've got kickboxing tomorrow.'

'Why don't you ask Scott to teach you if you're really interested, Jess?' Amy suggested. 'He's the absolute best. Better than Brodie—even though Brodie's the one who's made it his career.' She turned to Kate, looking quizzical. 'In fact, Kate, I don't know why *you* don't ask Scott to teach you. At least he lives in Sydney, so you'll get more than one lesson out of him.'

Kate busied herself snagging a server and ordering more drinks. By the time she'd done that, she had her poker face on. 'From what I've gathered, Scott doesn't sail any more.'

'That's true,' Willa said. 'You know, Weeping Reef was so beautiful, and we were all so excited to be there, but a lot of things went wrong. Things that…that changed us, I guess.'

'Ain't that the truth,' Amy murmured. And then she took a deep breath, seeming to shake off a thought. She smiled—very brightly. 'But that was then and this is now, so let's drink to moving on. Onwards and upwards, ladies. Onwards and upwards.'

The girls clinked glasses, although Kate wondered if her empty glass actually counted.

'The music is starting and they're opening the bar off the dance floor,' Jessica said. 'The crowd should spread out soon.' She looked at the packed bar area. 'I wonder if there's a rose-petal-sprinkler in amongst that lot who might be persuaded to ask me to dance.'

And then Jessica gasped, her eyes wide as saucers.

'Well, bite me!' she said. 'Maybe I *will* come along tomorrow, Kate. Because Brodie looks mighty hot.'

'Huh?' Amy swivelled in her seat and squealed.

Willa was the next to look. 'Oh, my God. I told Rob to join us here, but…but…how…?'

Kate turned very, very slowly as a cold finger of dread trailed its nail down her back.

Rob, Brodie…and Scott. Heading across the floor towards them.

CHAPTER FOURTEEN

'Look who I roped in!' Rob said as the three men reached the table.

And then everyone was standing, exclaiming, hugging, laughing. Even Jessica, who'd never met Brodie, was in there.

Everyone except Kate, who stayed in her seat with a fixed smile on her face, watching the reunion.

There was a general scrabbling for chairs while Brodie went off to the bar for beer and the next round of cocktails was delivered.

Rob sat and drew Willa onto his lap. 'Scott called to see if I wanted to go for a beer with him and Brodie, but I persuaded them to join us here instead,' he explained.

'I'm so glad you did,' Amy said. 'Because we were just talking about them.'

Scott sent Kate a brooding look, which started her heart thudding.

But all he said was, 'I'll go and find some extra chairs,' before stalking off.

Brodie was soon on his way back, carrying three beers as he cut across the small, still deserted dance floor rather than squeeze through the crush of drinkers spreading out from the bar.

He slid the beers onto the table and Rob snatched one up.

Jessica looked up at Brodie conspiratorially. 'We've been talking about our favourite romantic moments, Brodie. What do you think is better? Impressing a CFO with your business acumen—and no prizes for guessing who *that* one belongs to—strewn rose petals on a bed, a knight on a charger or *From Here to Eternity*?'

Brodie laughed. 'Are they the only options?'

Amy slapped her hand over Jessica's mouth—no doubt staving off any mention of dancing cheek to cheek in the Whitsundays.

'Can't take her anywhere,' Amy said, and quickly redirected the conversation.

Kate was relieved. Not only did she not want to hear the Chantal story again—not with Brodie at the table and Scott on approach—but she didn't want to let any red-blooded male into her guilty *From Here to Eternity* secret. And especially not Scott, who would laugh himself into apoplexy over it.

Scott had one of his false smiles in place as he handed a chair to Brodie. 'I had to promise to go back and have a drink with a group on a hen-night bender to get that chair, Brode!'

Brodie laughed as he took the chair. 'Don't pretend that's a hardship,' he said, and then grimaced an infinitesimal apology as his eyes flickered in Kate's direction.

Great. Brodie had seen her with Scott for all of ten minutes and yet he knew. Or maybe Scott had shared all the salacious details—perhaps with an offhand *And soon she'll be* all yours, *Brodie.*

Scott carefully didn't look at her—just positioned himself between Amy and Willa.

Brodie slotted his chair in beside Kate. 'Ready for tomorrow?' he asked, raising his voice a little over the rising sound of music that was being cranked up to encourage dancers to take to the floor.

'I'm still game if you are,' she said, leaning in close so she could be more easily heard.

'Oh, I'm game,' he said with an easy smile.

Such an *easy* smile. A *natural* smile. A smile that reached his eyes. Green eyes, like Scott's—but deep and warm, not cool and cautious.

Amy nudged her shoulder against Scott's. 'I told Kate she should have asked *you* for lessons.'

Scott cast Kate another brooding look and she felt herself blush almost by reflex. Everyone at the table would be working it out any minute if he kept that up.

'I sold my boat,' he said.

'Well, you could hire one, couldn't you?' Amy asked. 'What would it cost? To hire you and a boat and learn how to sail?'

'Well...' Scott said, and rubbed a jaw darkened by raspy shadow.

It was the first time Kate had ever seen him anything but clean-shaven. His eyes looked strained too. Tired. And she was an idiot, with no instinct for self-preservation, because she wanted to hug him, and kiss him, and tell him to take better care of himself—

'I'd say...' Scott began again, with another look at Kate '...five thousand dollars? Or the barter system is okay. Trade a service for a service.'

—and kill him. She wanted to *kill* him.

Amy looked shocked. 'Man, that's expensive.'

'But worth it,' Scott said. One more look at Kate, and then he turned to Willa to say something.

The conversation ebbed and flowed around Kate as, silent, she pondered the way her evening had started—four friends sharing their secret longings for romance. But Willa's was real. Whereas Kate's...? Pure Hollywood. Never going to happen.

And it was probably time she admitted that she wanted it to be real. Wanted what Willa had. Wanted someone to trust her with his life.

Because she *could* be trusted.

People trusted her with their lives every day. They trusted her to extricate them from bad marriages with a whole skin and the means to live. They trusted her to do the best thing for their children. They trusted her to find a way for them to achieve closure, and keep their dignity, and get a fair deal.

They trusted her...before moving on with their lives without her.

And that wasn't enough any more.

She wanted someone who trusted her but didn't *want* to move on with his life without her. She wanted someone complicated and creative, and strong and principled, and smart and funny, and sexy and…and…*hers*.

She wanted love. She wanted, specifically, *Scott Knight* to love her. Not just the scent, the taste, the feel of her…but the whole of her. Wanted to trust him with her life and wanted him to trust her with his.

She wanted him to tell her about growing up never feeling quite good enough, and she wanted to make sure he knew that he *was*. Good enough for anything—for everything.

She wanted *Scott* to tell her about Weeping Reef. About Chantal and Brodie. How he'd felt, what it had meant, what it had done to him to feel so betrayed, if it still ate at him.

She wanted to tell him she would never, ever hurt him like that. That she would never betray him. *Couldn't* betray him. That she—

'Kate?'

Brodie—pulling her back.

'Refill?' he asked, nodding at her glass, which was empty again.

'No,' she said, and tried to smile. 'And that's my last—so don't worry. There'll be no heave-hoing over the gunwales tomorrow.'

'It wouldn't be the first time I've held a girl's hair out of the way, so don't sweat it for my sake, Katie.'

Scott clunked his beer glass on the table. Loud enough to make Amy, sitting beside him, jump.

'Kate—not Katie,' he said. And then he turned back to Willa as though he hadn't just bowled that out loud and livid enough for everyone to marvel at, and asked, 'When's Luke coming home?'

After a stunned moment, Willa gathered herself enough to speak. 'No immediate plans, as far as I'm aware. He's in the middle of a deal in Singapore he won't tell me anything about. Confidential, apparently.'

'Confidential,' Amy repeated, but the tone of her voice—all dark, when Amy was basically the brightest, shiniest girl in the world—made Kate wonder if perhaps she wasn't the only one hitting the cocktails a little too hard.

'Yeah,' Willa said, a little uneasily. 'He's like a clam about stuff like that.'

Amy looked straight at Scott. 'But *you* know.'

'About Singapore?' Scott asked. 'Nope.'

'Not Singapore. I mean what happened at Weeping Reef.'

Kate wondered what she was missing and looked around at the others. Willa was looking startled—everyone else confused.

Scott half sighed, half laughed, winced. 'I think we all know what happened at Weeping Reef.'

'I *knew* he'd told you. You know—at Willa's party—when you said that…that thing about a gentleman never telling a lady's secrets.'

Nobody spoke.

'Amy,' Scott said into the awkward pause, 'if you think I have a lady's secret to tell—one that *doesn't* involve me getting up to no good with a hooker called Lorelei…' He waited while everyone at the table except a cringing Kate and a startled-looking Amy laughed. 'Then please fill me in. Otherwise I'm going to go and fulfil my obligation to that clutch of hens—or flock, or brood, or whatever the hell a group of chickens is called. The ones who donated a chair to our cause when I first arrived.'

He waited, watching Amy, who was blinking, stunned.

'Right, I'll take that as a no, then,' he said, and stood. 'Give me fifteen minutes,' he said to the group at large.

'Yeah—as if!' Jessica said as he was sucked into the crowd. 'It will only take him five minutes, max, to sort out his next one-night stand. He has the gift.'

But Amy was looking at Willa, dazed and confused. 'Luke really didn't…?'

Willa slid off Rob's lap and into Scott's vacated chair,

right next to Amy, and took Amy's hand. 'No, Amy. He really didn't.'

'Well...*wow!*' Amy said.

Brodie turned to Kate. 'We seem to be a little out of this loop, Kate. Shall we join the few brave souls venturing onto the dance floor?'

Kate had a feeling Scott wouldn't like her dancing with Brodie.

But, then again, Scott was in the process of picking up a drunken bed partner on a hen night.

And he'd told Brodie she was *all his.*

And Scott didn't love her.

And he never would.

And she wanted to die.

What was one dance stacked against all that?

'Sure,' she said.

Brodie led her onto the small dance floor. Without any hesitation—and completely ignoring the fact that every other couple on the floor was dancing without touching—he took Kate in his arms.

'What's going on?' Brodie asked, without preamble.

'What do you mean?'

'You and Scott. Am I going to get my teeth smashed in for dancing with you?'

'No. But I don't think the threat of that scares you or you wouldn't have asked me to dance, would you?'

No answer. He simply pulled her a little closer.

'So, Brodie, why *did* you ask me to dance?'

'Because I love Scott.'

'I don't—'

'And don't tell me you don't know what I mean, because you do.'

There was a pause as she silently acknowledged the truth of that. 'He won't care that I'm dancing with you. He's not the jealous type. Not with me anyway.' She sighed and settled her head on Brodie's comfortable shoulder. 'We're not...*meant.*'

'Why not?'

Kate ran through the reasons in her head and chose the least painful one she could think of. 'For a start, he's too young for me.'

She heard the laugh rumble through Brodie's chest. 'Scott hasn't been too young since he popped out of the womb—when he no doubt emerged *not* crying, just calmly looking around and wondering how to get fed without having to ask for help.'

Kate choked on a sudden giggle. 'That does sound like him.'

'Yep—everything calculated, everything his way, no drama, no demands, keep your distance. He has more self-control than anyone I've ever met. Too much.' Pause. 'I've only ever seen him lose it once.'

'I know about Chantal,' Kate said, looking up at him.

'Yeah, I figured you did. And if he told you that—'

'No,' Kate interrupted. 'He didn't tell me. He doesn't get personal. Not with me.'

'Ah.'

'Yes, *"ah".*'

'But you want him to?'

'What would be the point, when he's off picking some-one up for the night?'

'Except that he's not.'

'Well, who knows?'

'I do. Because if he was doing that he wouldn't be head-ing this way looking like he's about to deck me, would he?'

'What?' Kate squeaked, and Brodie spun them so she could see Scott as he approached.

'I wonder if he's about to cause the second scene of his life?' Brodie asked, not seeming at all concerned. 'Let's hope so.'

CHAPTER FIFTEEN

SCOTT HAD NO IDEA what he was doing, but he was doing it anyway.

He reached Kate and Brodie, then stood there like an idiot while he tried to contain the savage burst of possessiveness that was urging him to tear Kate out of Brodie's arms. This was beyond that drunken punch at Weeping Reef. Because this wasn't about Brodie, either as a love rival or as a Hugo substitute. This was about Kate and him. About wishing he *did* dance so it could be him dancing with her. Wishing it was *him* teaching her to sail. About hating himself because of all the things he wasn't—but wanting to demand, anyway, what the *hell* she thought she was doing dancing with another man when she belonged to him.

He barely noticed Brodie melting away as he reached for Kate, yanked her into his arms and kissed her. Right there on the dance floor. A scorching kiss, which he hoped said *I want you*, but suspected said something else. Something about need and desperation and all the things he didn't want to risk.

When he stopped, pulled back, looked down at her, she shivered. He felt it rip through him as though they were connected.

'I think that qualifies as a PDA,' she said.

'That had nothing to do with affection. That kiss was not *affectionate*, Kate.'

'That kiss is not going to lead to sex either.'

'Yes, it is.'

'No. We have an appointment, and it's not for tonight.'

'We can negotiate, remember?'

'You don't negotiate. You do whatever the hell you want, whenever you want.'

'That's because your rules are stupid.'

'You agreed to them.'

'I shouldn't have.'

'But you did. And now you've gone and broken the confidentiality clause.' She nodded towards their table. 'Because your friends just saw you kiss me.'

His only response was to grab her hand and drag her off the dance floor, out of the bar, into the night, around the corner into an alleyway that was only a step above Ellington Lane in terms of desolation. Without a word he took her in his arms again, kissed her almost savagely. He wanted her so much—so *much*.

Her hands grabbed the front of his shirt, clutching fistfuls of it, anchoring her as she kissed him back, and he thought, *Thank God*. She wanted him. She still wanted him. Everything else would fall into place as long as that fact held. Because without it why would she keep seeing him?

There was a burst of sound as the bar's main doors opened, disgorging a group of people into the night, and sanity returned. The doors closed again. A low conversation, a trill of laughter from the departing patrons. Scott pulled back, waiting to see if he and Kate would be discovered, but the group passed by. All was quiet again.

And Scott suddenly felt utterly, utterly miserable.

He stepped away, shoved his hands in his hair, looked at Kate.

'What was *that* about?' she asked—as usual, going straight to the point in the way he just bloody loved.

'I wanted to kiss you, that's all.' Could he sound any more defensive?

'So what happens if I ask you—now—to come inside and dance with me, in public, in front of your friends?'

Tight, fraught pause. Scott stuck his hands in his pockets. 'I don't dance.'

'No, you *don't* dance, do you? But that doesn't mean *I*

don't, Scott, if I'm lucky enough to be asked. And I *was* dancing. Why did you drag me out here?'

'Because—' He broke off with a muffled curse.

'Because…I was dancing with *Brodie*, perhaps?'

One heavy heartbeat…two, three.

And then, 'Why is that a problem, Scott?'

No answer. Because how could he explain without revealing everything that was wrong with him? All the reasons she would soon find someone better—whether it was Brodie or that barrister or someone else? How could he tell her that he needed to push it? Push it while he still had it in him to get over her when the inevitable happened?

'Do you think I prefer him?' Kate persisted.

He shrugged as his hands dug a little deeper into his pockets. 'If you do, that's okay. Women…lots of women…do.'

He said the words but his heart was threatening to leap into his brain and cut off his blood supply, oxygen, his synapse control—everything. Because it *wasn't* okay. It would kill him.

'Not *lots of women*, Scott,' she said. '*Chantal*. And that's what this is all about, isn't it? Chantal. The only woman who ever got to you. Enough to make you lose that prized control.'

Scott registered the fact that she knew about Chantal. Who'd told her? Did it even matter? He tested that in his brain. No, it didn't. Because Chantal didn't matter. It had been *Brodie* who'd mattered all those years ago, not Chantal. And now…only Kate mattered. *Only Kate.*

'I'll teach you to sail,' he said, which was so far from an adequate response as to be classified as a non sequitur.

'You don't have a boat, remember? And I don't have five thousand dollars since I ripped up your cheque—which, in case you're too stupid to realise it, was only ever a Play Time prop. So no need to trade sailing lessons for my services like I'm a *real* prostitute. I'm already under contract. You're getting the goods for free. Until the twenty-eighth, anyway.'

She turned to walk away and his temper surged, hot and

wild. His hands came out of his pockets and he grabbed her, spun her, gripping her upper arms, furious. 'Don't talk about yourself like that.'

'Then stop making me feel like that by trading me to your friends,' she shot back. '*"She's all yours."* Remember?'

'All you have to do is tell him no. No, you're not going sailing tomorrow. Tell him, Kate,' Scott said, wanting to explode with the emotions churning in his gut, but hanging on…and on, and on.

'I *am* going sailing tomorrow,' she said. 'As planned. Because he *offered*, without having to be shamed into it. But don't worry, Scott. If anything happens between me and Brodie I'll advise you. As I expect you to tell me if you hook up with one of those giggly hens. And that will be that, won't it? Agreement null and void, as per the contract. Okay?'

They stared at each other. Scott's hands unclenched, slipped down her arms to her hands, held. The words were there in his chest. *Not okay. Don't do it to me. Don't. Please, please don't.* Choking him.

'Kate. Oh, God, Kate. I just—'

But the bar doors opened again and Scott let go, stepped back, re-jamming his hands in his pockets at the sudden burst of sound. People were walking past, talking, laughing.

And up popped his shield, like some automatic reflex. 'Okay,' he said.

'*Okay?*' she said, incredulous. And then, 'Okay…'

Her eyes closed.

Long moment, and then she opened her eyes. 'I don't understand any of this. Why did you let Rob talk you into coming here when you knew I'd be here? It's not what we're about, is it? Drinks with friends?'

'I wanted—' Stop. Swallow. *Confess.* 'I wanted to see you.'

'You're seeing me on Sunday. At noon. Remember?'

'I remember. But who'll be opening the door? Kate? Officer Cleary? Or Lorelei?'

'Who do you *want* to see, Scott?'

Silence. Because the answer had stuck in his throat. The way words always did.

He saw her shoulders slump, as if she was defeated. Knew he wasn't handling this. Wasn't handling *her*. Wasn't handling *anything*.

'Surprise me,' he said, and forced a smile. His *I'm cool with that* smile.

Except he *wasn't* cool with it. He wanted her to call him on what he'd said. To fight with him. Rage at him. Slap him if she had to. To demand more. *More!* To tell him that she *deserved* more and she *wanted* more. And she wanted it from *him*. To say, *So step up to the plate, Scott Knight, and if you can't give it to me I'll find it somewhere else. I'll find someone else. Someone...else.*

Say it—say it, Kate. You want someone else. Say it!

But she gave him smile for cool smile instead. 'Fine,' she said. 'I'll make sure it's memorable for you.'

And then she patted her hair into place. Twitched at her dress.

'But now I'm going to go back inside to get my things. I've had a big week. A bad week. And I need to go home.'

He wanted to take her hands again, but he couldn't seem to get them out of his pockets. 'Tell me. What happened with the case?'

She looked at him. And the tears in her eyes almost undid him. But when she spoke her voice was like crystal. Clear and smooth and cold.

'No fireside chats, remember?'

'But I—'

'Stop, Scott. Just *stop*. I came out to relax with a few girl-friends and instead I'm standing in a dark alley with a man who's not saying anything that makes sense. I just want to go in, pay my bill, grab my things and leave. You go back to that hen party, and text me before Sunday if you've been unfaithful.' Short, strange laugh. 'How quaint that sounds. Let's say, instead, if you've adhered to the clause.'

And with that, she stalked out of the alleyway.

By the time Scott had himself enough under control to return to the table, Kate had been and gone.

He picked up the fresh beer that was waiting for him because Brodie, who had his back like in the old days, had known he'd need one.

'Want to borrow my boat in the morning?' Brodie asked.

Scott smiled—his *all okay here* smile. 'No, I'm good. She's all yours.' *Oh, God, no!* He'd said it again. *All yours.*

'I think we both know, Scott, that she's all *yours*. But if you'll take my advice you won't take too long to claim her— because Kate doesn't strike me as the type to wait forever.'

CHAPTER SIXTEEN

KATE WOKE ON Sunday with full-blown jitters.

Because she didn't have a clue what she was going to offer Scott for Play Time at noon.

It was almost more than her tired, slightly sunburned body could manage just to get out of bed, let alone plan a fantasy, because yesterday's sailing lesson had been the most full-on physical three hours she'd ever spent.

Sailing was as freeing, as exhilarating, as wonderful as she'd always thought it would be—with an excellent side benefit: all that hauling of sheets and dodging of booms, being ordered around and shoved all over the deck by Brodie and his two cohorts, had left her with no time to think about Scott. Or about their upcoming Play Time either.

The guys had taken her out for a congratulatory drinking session afterwards, because apparently she had what it took, and by the time Kate had got home, she'd been so tired she'd fallen into bed.

She'd slept for a full three hours before thoughts of Scott had niggled her into wakefulness. And then had come the night-long tossing and turning she was learning to expect.

Fractured sleep, painful dreams, tortured thoughts. Wondering how Scott had felt, knowing she was on the water with his best friend. Rethinking every look, every word from Friday night. Trying to figure out what was behind the anger Scott refused to unleash—was it the way he felt about her, or residual mistrust from the eight-year-old Chantal/Brodie situation? Hoping he hadn't—*please, please, please*—voided their contract by touching another woman.

After all that it was no wonder she was devoid of ideas.

Arabian nights, pirate and tavern wench, boss and secretary—all of which she'd considered—just seemed stupid.

How she wished she'd never thought of writing fantasies into the contract. She hated Play Time. *Hated* it!

So much so that in a fit of pique—yes, *pique*!—she decided to wear her most complicated dress. Buttons *and* zips *and* ties, with an exotic fold or two. An origami nightmare of a dress. Because Scott *deserved* to have to fight his way through to her for a change, rather than have her laying it all out for him to take.

He'd said the first time they met that for her he could get a little 'gladiatorial'—so let him prove it by fighting his way past her dress! In fact, she would make it harder. She would blindfold him! And what was more, she would give him a time limit.

That was a good enough Play Time for her.

Scott buzzed on the dot of noon—he was nothing if not punctual—and she let him into the building without waiting to hear his voice.

'We only have an hour,' Kate said, all brisk and business-like as she opened the door to him, holding two silk scarves at the ready.

His eyes narrowed. 'Why?'

'Nothing to do with Brodie, if that's what you're wondering.'

'I'm not wondering. Are you wondering?'

'About Brodie?'

He just looked at her.

'Oh, do you mean am I wondering about you and the hens on Friday night?' she asked, and eked out a tinkling laugh. 'No. You would have texted me, wouldn't you, if anything had happened?' She was forcing the panic back. 'And any-way…well, *pacta sunt servanda*, right? Agreements must be kept. And as I recall, that was your sticking point. Fidelity.'

'Pacta sunt servanda,' he repeated. 'You *do* remember how that legal talk turns me on, don't you?'

Her breath caught in her throat. 'Yes.'

'Is that why you're doing it?'

'The more turned on you are, the faster we'll be, right?'

He didn't like that—she could tell by the way his whole face tightened. He walked past her and laid a flat parcel on her dining table.

'Stand still while I do this,' she said, coming up behind him.

And, although he stiffened, he let her tie the scarf over his eyes.

'Play Time,' she announced.

The set of his mouth was grim as she led him carefully into the bedroom, over to the bed. 'Sit,' Kate said.

But Scott did more than sit. He flopped onto his back, lying there as though he didn't give a damn what she did to him, and Kate hesitated, wondering if he didn't want her today. If he didn't want her any more, period.

Pulse jittering, she looked at his body, laid out on the bed for her, wondering how she would be able to bear that…and saw that he was hard. She hadn't even touched him and he was aroused—whether he wanted to be or not.

It took the edge off her sudden panic to know that whatever his *I give up* attitude was about, it wasn't a lack of desire. She could work with that. She would make this so good for him he wouldn't be able to pretend he didn't want her.

'I'm going to blindfold myself now,' she told him, knowing how disorientating it must be for a control freak like Scott not to know what was happening. 'No peeking today—by either of us. And no speaking either.'

'No—?' Short, tense pause. 'No *speaking*, Kate?'

'No. Just…feeling…'

Scott's lips tightened but he said nothing.

And then Kate tied her own scarf and felt her way onto the bed. She lay next to him, turned to him, kissed him. A long, lush moan of a kiss. Not being able to see, she was even more conscious than usual of the uncompromising firmness of his mouth as he stayed stock-still for her to explore. The warmth of it, the taste, the way it fitted so perfectly against her own.

Slowly the tension left him, and at last he kissed her back, his tongue sliding into her mouth, and then he was taking over, reaching everywhere. Thank *God*.

A moment later his hands were wandering over her fully clothed body. Traversing the cotton of her dress. Pausing, testing, assessing the fastenings, the barriers.

Kate's task was easier. She slid her hands under his T-shirt, smoothing them over his chest. She loved his chest. The breadth and strength of it, the texture of his warm skin, the spread of hair. The picture of him, flat on his back on her bed, was so strong in her mind…but the fact she couldn't see it with her eyes somehow made the drug of touching him more potent. As if she could reach right through his chest and into his heart with nothing but the pads of her exploring fingers.

A push, a nudge, and his T-shirt was up, over his head, off. She checked quickly that the scarf was still secure around his eyes, and then her hands moved to his jeans. Unbuttoning, unzipping as his breathing turned harsh and laboured. She loved the way his breaths came like that when he was excited, almost past bearing but trying to control it—control himself, control everything.

She straddled him, facing his feet—which might have felt weird if they hadn't both been masked, but now felt perfect. Her core was on his warm skin, just above the band of his boxer briefs. Just that was enough for her to long to have him inside her. She started pushing his jeans down his legs, hands stroking as she leaned further forward with each push. She loved his legs. Long, hard, strong, the perfect amount of hair. Down, down, down. And then—*stop*.

She'd forgotten about his sneakers. Well, blindfolded or not, she could undo a shoe. She fumbled with the laces, wrenched the sneakers off, threw them. They landed on the floor with a soft thud. Next she pushed his jeans off, threw them too. Started to turn around.

But Scott kept her exactly where she was with a hand on her back. She got the message and stopped, on her knees, one either side of his hips. Stayed…waited. What was he going to do?

And then the hand on her back was gone and both Scott's hands were under her dress, reaching between her spread thighs, snagging against the French knickers she'd put on today before she'd come up with a plan that meant he wouldn't actually *see* the frothy pink lace.

He didn't seem to care about the lace, because his fingers were impatient, almost rough, as he yanked the knickers aside, his fingers sliding into her drenching wetness, in and out, until her breaths were nothing more than rasps and she was trembling. She felt so hot, so lush, aching as those fingers continued to dip in and out of her while the fingers of his other hand joined the action, circling her clitoris, precise, constant, inexorable.

She hadn't removed his underwear, but that didn't stop him thrusting hard against her bottom as he circled and slipped and probed every millimetre of her sex until she was coming in a luscious roll.

She didn't know how it had happened, but a moment later she found herself flipped onto her back. She waited, breathless, for what Scott would do—regretting the damned dress, deciding she would help with her own unwrapping.

But before she could lift a finger to even one zipper, Scott had gripped the cotton at her neck and torn the dress right down the front, spreading the two halves wide.

'Scott…' she whispered, shocked.

'No talking,' he said, and reached for her bra straps, accurate despite the blindfold.

He yanked them down her arms until her breasts were bared. Unerringly, his mouth found her nipples, sucking, licking, building the pressure from barely there to strong and demanding, unrelenting as his cotton-clad erection strained against her.

She reached down to try to push his underwear off him, clumsy because of her bra straps, but he knocked her hands aside and kept up the suckling. Next moment he was scooting down her body, between her legs. The French knickers were shoved down and his mouth was there, licking fast and frantically, and she was coming again with a loud cry.

He kept his mouth there through the last undulation of her hips and then he came back up her body, kissing her almost brutally. He fumbled with the scarf over her eyes, ripping it away. Rising up over her, on his knees, he tore off his own blindfold. Stared down at her for a scorching moment.

Before Kate could reach for him he was off the bed, throwing his clothes on helter-skelter.

'But— But— What about you?'

'Owe me,' he said, zipping up his jeans.

'I can do it now.'

'You should have grabbed a condom before the blindfolds went on. Because now I've ripped the masks off, Play Time's over. We're seeing…we're talking. And that's not in the rules for today, is it? You don't want to *talk* to me today. You don't want to *see* me today. I'd say you didn't even really want me to *touch* you, or you wouldn't have worn that chastity belt of a dress. You wanted it over with *quickly* today.'

He grabbed his sneakers, shoved his feet inside them, yanked on the laces.

'Well, you're done—all sorted, all serviced with time to spare—and now I'm going.'

'Scott…'

But he was out of the room, and her curse was floating behind him.

'Scott—wait,' she said as she got off the bed, impatiently shedding her ruined dress, wrenching up her bra.

The door slammed before she was even out of the bedroom.

He was gone.

Eyes swimming, she walked over to the dining table, picked up the parcel he'd left there. Opened the brown paper. Removed a...a *plaque*? Yes, a simple metal plaque. Black type on dull silver. Two words: *Castle Cleary*.

Her swimming eyes overflowed.

To hell with Play Time, Scott thought savagely as he got into his car. And to hell with being made to feel like a male prostitute with an allocated time slot.

Not that the whole blindfold experience hadn't been intense. He'd been insane with need by the end of it. So needy it had made no sense to run out when he did. She would have serviced him even without the blindfolds.

Serviced him.

And didn't that say it all?

She would have *serviced* him. The way he'd *serviced* her.

Scott Knight, Escort Service, at your beck and call.

So what? his sane self asked.

It was perfect, wasn't it? Exactly what he'd wanted? A sex contract. Month to month. No strings. No emotions. Complete control. No pretending they were forever. No need to call her unless it was to schedule a hot bout of sex. No deep and meaningful conversations. No conversations at all, lately—not with Lorelei, not with Officer Cleary. And not with Kate.

And today not only no speaking, but no looking either!

Just feeling—which was a good enough euphemism for *just sex*.

Just sex.

Perfect.

And he was a freaking idiot not to just take that and run with it.

Scott pulled out his phone. Stabbed the buttons.

Play Time, my house, Tuesday, 7 p.m.

Half a minute later, back came a reply.

Fine.

'Right,' he said out loud to his face in the rearview mirror.

But something about his face wasn't normal. He looked like a freaking psycho killer!

Well, to hell with that too! He was *not* going to see that every time he glanced in the rearview mirror on the drive home. He'd have a crash if he had to see that.

He had to calm the hell down.

Cursing, he banged out of the car, strode across to the marina, focused on the boats.

Which made him feel even crazier. And just miserable again.

Kate had had her first sailing lesson yesterday. With Brodie. How had it gone? What had they talked about? Fireside chats aplenty with Brodie, for sure. Because Brodie was easy to talk to—easier than Scott. Easier, kinder. Better all round.

Everything inside Scott clenched—including the growl that he wouldn't let loose from his chest.

And then he put his face in his hands—because the sight of the boats was suddenly unbearable.

CHAPTER SEVENTEEN

KATE WAS PREPARED for the Monday morning *What the hell was that kiss about?* calls from Willa and Amy. She offered up a perfectly nuanced laugh as she blamed the lethal combination of Scott's beer and her Manhattans, positioning it as a Dirty Martini Barnaby moment gone a step too far. And if the girls didn't sound exactly convinced, at least they let the subject drop.

She was *less* prepared for Deb's darting, anxious eyes as she kept a steady flow of peppermint tea—her favourite stress remedy—pouring into Kate's office—while very carefully *not* asking about 'that nice Scott Knight'. Not that Deb had to ask; Kate was convinced she had psychic powers.

And she was not *at all* prepared for her mother's visit on Tuesday morning.

Madeline Cleary swept into Kate's office the way she swept through life: grandly, wearing a caftan, hot-pink lipstick and high heels.

She took a seat, fixing Kate with one of her *don't mess with me* stares. 'Okay, Kate, what's this Deb's been telling me?'

Deb! Psychic and *traitor*!

'"This"'? Kate asked, closing the door sharply—knowing it would drive Deb crazy not being able to listen in, which served her right.

'Scott Knight,' her mother said.

'He's an architect.'

'Well, isn't that lovely? Much more interesting than a barrister. But not really the pertinent fact at the moment, is it, Kate? Don't bother with any of your legal obfuscation. Just tell me what's happening.'

'No.'

'Okay, then bring him to dinner on Sunday and I'll ask him instead.'

'That won't be happening. It's not like that with us. I mean the…the family thing. It's just…just…' The words trailed off and she shrugged.

Her mother looked at her—very long, very hard. 'It's just that he's the one, perhaps?'

Kate tried—failed—to laugh. 'Nothing that romantic.'

'So *make* it romantic.'

'You can't make these things happen.'

'Not if you're pussy-hearted. Which, of course, is *not* the way I raised my daughters. I raised lionesses.' She leaned forward. 'Kate, remember when I tried to dissuade you from going into family law?'

Eye-roll. 'Yes.'

'Not because I don't like lawyers—'

Another eye-roll. 'Although you don't!'

'But because you're so tender-hearted. I knew you'd be running yourself ragged, fighting for the downtrodden and then bleeding all over the place when you lost a case.' She sat back again. 'And do you remember what you told me to do?'

Kate smiled—it blossomed despite her hideous mood. 'I told you to shove it.'

Her mother beamed at her. 'And I was so proud of you.'

Kate ran her hands over her face, laughing helplessly. 'You're a weirdo, Mum.'

'It's an artistic thing. So what?'

'So I love you.'

'And I love you. And I think you deserve a reward for all the crap you put up with day after day. And if he's the reward you want, then you're going to have him.'

'He doesn't want…that. The whole forever thing.'

'From what I hear, he's had plenty of what *he* wants.'

Arrgghh. Going to kill Deb. Boil her in a vat of peppermint tea.

'So, Kate, it's time for what *you* want. Which just might turn out to be what he wants too.'

'He doesn't.'

'How do you know? Have you asked him?'

'No, of course not.'

'Why "of course not"? Because he's a boy and they have to ask first? Don't make me slap you. Just *ask* him.'

Silence.

'Kate, the reason I was so proud of you that day when you told me so eloquently to shove it was because you threw it all at me. How you felt, why you felt it, what it meant to you. You said you would move heaven and hell to do it. And that if it all came to nothing, or you couldn't hack it, at least you'd have no regrets about not *trying*. And, really, Kate? If it's *you* asking for something, fighting for something…'

She smiled—a smile so completely proud and understanding and just so *family* Kate wanted to cry. 'Well, Kate, who would ever say no to you?'

Who would ever say no to you?

Oh, God. God! Scott would say no. *He* would.

'So, Kate, *tell him*. What you feel. Why you feel it. What he means to you. And move heaven and hell. Because, of all of my daughters, *you* can. And then, whatever happens, at least you'll have no regrets.' She paused again, shrugged. 'The alternative is that I tell your father what he's done to you—and he and Aristotle have been playing with a new set of throwing knives, so I'd prefer not to go that route. At least not yet.'

Kate arrived at Scott's on Tuesday ten minutes late.

She stayed in her car for another ten minutes, with her mother's words going through her mind. *Tell him, tell him, tell him.*

But she couldn't help feeling it would be like pulling the rug out from under him. *I said it was only going to be sex, Scott, but it's love.*

What would he say?

Big sigh. Because she had no idea.

He'd sent so many mixed signals her way she was beyond knowing what he expected of her, what he wanted from her, how he felt about her. He'd been everything from distant to demanding, from impassioned to indifferent. From flippant to furious. Agreeing to the rules—and breaking them.

The way he'd looked at her in that alley on Friday night, when he'd taken her hands in his—that was not about sex. And that last Play Time, when he'd been so angry with her—irrational, emotional…

Wasn't that a bit like love?

She sucked in a breath, because just saying that in her head made her heart flutter. Running a hand over her stomach, which was similarly fluttery, she wondered, maybe, if she *should* ask him.

But *after* Play Time. Because if Play Time involved her getting into a PVC cat suit or wielding some kind of implement…? Well, she couldn't see herself talking about love after a dose of kink.

Sighing, she started to push the intercom button—but Scott opened the door before the chime even sounded. He took her in his arms, kissed her as though he'd been waiting a year and was starving for the taste of her.

And *everything* in her fluttered. Nervous and hopeful and a little bit terrified.

Releasing her slowly, Scott gestured for her to move into the house, and she was struck again by the magnificence of what he'd achieved—even more so today, when she was seeing it as Kate, who'd been invited, not Lorelei, who'd invited herself.

It was stylish, lavish, unusual. A manifestation of all those parts that made Scott who he was. The coolness, the control, the hidden fiery core.

Kate cleared her throat. 'So… Play Time?'

He put his arm around her, led her into what she supposed was the living room—or living *space*, more correctly, since there were no internal walls, only strategically placed columns.

'Yep,' he said. 'I'm calling it "The Architect and the Lawyer".'

She halted as her hopes started to soar. 'That sounds… normal.'

'Ah, but with a twist. The way I'm seeing it is that the architect gives the lawyer a tour of his house. Along the way the lawyer tries to find a legal term appropriate for each space—extra points for Latin. And if the lawyer likes what she sees, she gets to touch the architect. And if the architect likes what the lawyer says…same deal. He gets to touch her. And then the architect—because he is multi-talented—prepares dinner. And they eat. And drink wine. And then, if all that touching has meant anything at all, they go upstairs to bed and negotiate the rollover of their contract for another month.'

'Oh,' she said as her hopes stopped soaring and started plummeting. The contract. One more month. Not exactly forever.

Scott took her briefcase, threw it onto his glamorous coffee-coloured couch with no regard for the potential damage its buckles could do to the fabric, and slowly turned her to the living area. 'So—what do you think?' he asked.

She tried to smile. 'I guess I'll start with…*ab initio*.'

'Well, I'm going to have to kiss you for that.'

'Do you even know what it means?'

'No.'

And then he drew her close and kissed her cheek. Just her cheek…but she felt it tingle all the way through her body.

'So what *does* it mean?' he asked when he released her.

'"From the beginning",' she said. 'It's commonly used to refer to the time a contract, statute, deed or…or marriage becomes legal.' *Oh, God—why had she mentioned marriage?* She cleared her throat. 'But in this instance we'll use it for the start of the house tour.'

'Suits me,' Scott said. '*Ab initio*. We can use it for the start of our new month too.'

'Hmm…' Kate said. A vague, *nothing* noise. 'Where to next?'

'Library—which, you will be interested to note, used to be an altar.'

She could already see it, and walked slowly across the wooden floor and up the three steps. So beautiful. Coloured rugs. A fireplace—unlit in the heat of February. Books nestling in custom-made shelves; armchairs—some leather, some fabric—low wooden tables. She turned to face the main space, looking out at the expansive floor, partitioned into discrete zones via the columns—all spectacularly clean and modern, which made the library feel like an oasis of plush comfort.

'It could do with a few of your mother's paintings, but otherwise what do you think?' Scott asked.

Mother. Her mother. *Tell him, tell him.* 'Umm…' She turned to him. '*Ad coelum*.'

Scott drew her in and kissed her eyelids. First one, then the other.

'If you like it…aren't you going to touch me?' he asked, all husky.

Kate reached a hand up, cupped his face, ran her thumb over his cheekbone. 'Want to know what it means?' she asked.

'Yes, as soon as you touch me again—you owe me for the living room.'

She brought up her other hand and now both hands cradled his face. She leaned up, kissed him gently on the mouth. And then she smiled into his eyes.

'To the sky. It's actually abbreviated from *cuius est solum eius est usque ad coelum et ad inferos*—which basically means whoever owns the soil owns that space, all the way up to heaven and down to hell. And this is just heavenly. Which seems apt for a converted church.'

'You've got no idea how much you are turning me on, Kate.'

'That's the whole idea of Play Time, isn't it?'

He frowned slightly, but said nothing. Simply took her arm and continued the tour.

Scott showed her all over the masterpiece that was the lower floor. And it was obvious why his renown as an architect was growing.

The huge arched panels of stained glass juxtaposed against the ultra-modern use of materials and neutral colours in most of the spaces were startling and lovely. The structure of the zones, flowing one into the next, was incredible. Scott's stark office and the state-of-the-art kitchen and guest bathroom were top-notch contemporary. The surprising pops of colour, like the scarlet staircase and the chartreuse relaxation nook off a plant-filled atrium, were brilliantly eccentric. How could such disparate elements combine into something so blow-your-head-off gorgeous? But that was…*Scott*.

Kate had to concentrate hard in order to be able to spit out Latin legal phrases, only to have her thoughts scatter every time Scott chose a different part of her to kiss. It was agonising, this falling in love. Feeling it dig itself more deeply inside her with every gentle, lavishing touch of Scott's fingers, his mouth, on her lips, her cheeks, her ears, her eyebrows—her damned *eyebrows*!—and her hair. Wishing so hard it meant something, the way his eyes closed, the way he held his breath as she touched him in turn. Shoulders, hands, neck, chest.

She was in torment by the time they circled back to the library, where Scott settled her with a drink while he finished preparing dinner. He was so jaunty as he left her—even whistling, as though he had everything he could possibly want.

But then, Scott *did* have everything he wanted. *Exactly* what he wanted. *She* was the one who didn't have what she wanted. And she still had no idea how to get it—except to ask for it…and risk losing even the little of him she had.

Kate didn't know how long had passed when Scott came to escort her through to the dining area. But she could feel time just generally slipping away. Four days until the twenty-eighth of February. When their contract would be terminated—or rolled over.

Scott held out a chair for her at the sleek wooden table and waited for her to sit.

'You didn't have to cook dinner,' Kate said.

'Well, you see, Kate, the fifty-fifty rule wasn't working for me. So this—' charming little shrug '—is my way of taking you to dinner. And before you tell me I'm breaking the rules, I'm going to remind you that extras are allowed in Play Time.' He sat opposite her. 'Cucumber soup. Perfect for a Sydney summer.'

But Kate was beyond taste as she silently filled her spoon, raised it to her mouth, swallowed. Time after time. Until her bowl was empty.

Scott—who'd done an excellent job of keeping up a flow of small talk—cleared the plates, then returned with something that looked so delicious Kate's heart sank. He'd taken such care—but how was she supposed to eat it when her heart had swelled so gigantically it threatened to choke her?

'Korean-style pork tenderloin with wild and brown rice pilaf and steamed pea pods,' Scott announced.

As Kate doggedly forced the food down Scott explained a house design he was currently working on. Presumably she offered appropriate rejoinders, because he didn't make an issue of her lack of vocal enthusiasm.

But then, why would he? It wasn't *conversation* he wanted.

He cleared the plates a second time, and while he was gone Kate had a mini-meltdown, remembering her mother's words. *Make it romantic.* How did a person turn a contract into something romantic? *Move heaven and hell.* How? What was the trigger? What would it take to make him love her?

And then he was back, carrying a tray. On the tray was a plate piled high with cookies of some kind and two exquisite boxes—one pink, one purple—decorated with fluttery fairies, shimmering with glitter, finished off with gauzy bows.

'Whoopie pies,' Scott said, depositing the tray in front of Kate and taking the seat beside her.

Unable to stop herself, Kate reached for one of the boxes, ran suddenly trembling fingers over the top, pulled the end of the ribbon through her fingertips.

'Do you like those boxes?' Scott asked.

She looked at him, said nothing.

'They're for Maeve and Molly. Because...' He shrugged, blushed. 'Well, you know... I spoke to them about baking whoopie pies and I... Well, since I didn't know when I was going to see them again, and I was baking anyway, I thought they... Ah, hell, I thought they'd like them. That's all. And I saw the boxes in a store near my office, so I...' He cleared his throat. 'I bought them. No big deal.'

Nice and defiant. Still blushing.

And everything surged in Kate—wrenching at her heart, racing through her blood, shattering every thought in her brain...flooding her with absolute crazy love. She was insanely, wildly in love with him.

She couldn't pretend any more. Not for one more moment.

And the next moment of her life started precisely *now*.

'Hugo,' she said.

CHAPTER EIGHTEEN

SCOTT REELED BACK in his chair. 'What's he got to do with anything?'

'I don't know, Scott. Why don't you tell me what he has to do with you, with us, or indeed with anything? Because you've told me precious little so far. So—Hugo.'

'Oh, I get it. Is this—? This is about…about Play Time. Stopping Play Time, right?'

'Yes, Scott, it is.'

'But…why? What was so bad? Do you want to…to go back and start again?'

'No.'

He blinked. 'Okay, then, let's skip it altogether and just go upstairs and—'

'Hugo,' Kate said again.

He tried to smile, but didn't nail it. 'You don't know what I was going to suggest.'

Kate didn't bother even trying to smile. 'The fact that you said we should go upstairs—to bed, no doubt—tells me all I need to know. It tells me we don't have a relationship.'

'Sure we do.'

'No, Scott, we don't. We have a contract.'

'You're the one who wanted the contract.'

'Semantics. With or without the signed piece of paper, we have an *arrangement*. An arrangement is *not* a relationship. And if you're happy with that then I'm calling "Hugo". As in *enough*. No more Play Time. No more anything.'

Scott shoved a hand into his hair. 'Kate, if it's the subject of my brother that's bothering you—'

'Didn't you listen? Hugo—as in *I'm finished*.'

'—he has nothing to do with us.' Right over the top of her. 'I never thought you'd meet him.'

'Well, I did meet him, Scott, so how about you explain now?'

Silence. Scott's jaw tightened.

'Scott?'

'You're the smartest person I've ever met, Kate. I'm sure you worked it all out the night of the architect awards. Why do you need to wring the words out of me?'

Kate stared at him.

He stared back.

And then he shoved *both* his hands into his hair. 'Dammit— all right. It's no big deal.'

He took a moment. Placed his hands on the table, palms down. Very specific. Controlling them.

'Very simply: my brother was the perfect child. Better than me at school, better than me at sport, better than me at everything. My parents let me know it in a thousand ways when we were growing up. And when Hugo hit the doctor target…? Big bonus points, there. Now he's hit all the personal targets too—getting married, providing grandchildren. Long story short—Hugo is *family* all the way. And I'm…*not*. I'm number two. All the way.'

Kate reached for his hand but Scott pulled it back, out of the touch zone.

'All the way,' he repeated. 'Want an example, Kate? What about that time I was in the Whitsundays, goofing off, teaching holidaymakers to sail, making a fool of myself over a girl who didn't love me? What do you think my brother was doing?' But the question was rhetorical. 'He was one-upping me spectacularly by sailing solo around the world.'

'So what?' Kate asked, but it was hard to get that out because she wanted to cry.

'So *what*?' Scott laughed—harsh and awful. 'So sailing was *my* thing. Why did he have to take that too? I swear, if he knew I liked cooking he'd go and get himself a publishing deal for a cookbook.'

'Hugo didn't win the architecture prize. You did.'

'Wait until next year's awards,' Scott said. 'He'll pull a rabbit out of someone's hat.'

'Exactly, Scott! Out of someone *else's* hat! Unlike you, wearing your *own* hat. Because you can't tell me you simply follow blindly—not your parents, not your brother, not anyone. Otherwise you'd be a doctor like the rest of your family—you're certainly smart enough.'

'There's no mystery there, Kate. I just wanted to be an architect.'

'I know that. And I know why. Because it's *you*. Creativity—and order. The perfect career for *you*! And I think your brother hates how good you are at it. Because you can bet that although you could be a doctor if you wanted to—'

'Not as good as Hugo.'

'Maybe…maybe not—but you could be *some* kind of doctor. Hugo, however, could never be *any* kind of architect.'

'You can't possibly tell that.'

'Sure I can—because he wasn't the one in the navy blue tux that night. He doesn't have it. *It*. That thing you have. And what does it tell you that he didn't even have the grace to come over and congratulate you when you won that award?'

Scott said nothing.

'That he was jealous,' Kate said. '*Is* jealous. Of you.'

Scoffing laugh. 'He has nothing to be jealous of.'

'Really? Because the way I see it, you have something Hugo wants badly but will never, ever have. I'll bet your parents don't have it either. I'll bet none of them even understands it—which is why it's three against one in the Knight family. You have creativity, and charisma, and wit, and decency, and…and adventure in your soul, and so much more. *That's* why you went to the Whitsundays, and why Hugo had to make do with what he *thought* was one better. Except it *wasn't* one better. He had to *follow* you to one-up you. And he had to one-up you because that's the only way he can feel better than you. He can't bear your success because he wants it *all*—all for himself. He can't *be* you, so he *steals* from you. But he can't steal the one thing he really wants because that would make him…you. And, no matter what he tries, he never *will* be you.'

Scott shook his head, wearing one of those smiles that meant nothing.

'And the sailing thing?' she said urgently. 'I'd tell you to make it your thing again, if it bothers you, but you don't *have* to make it your thing. Because it *is* your thing. It always was—and it will be waiting for you when you're ready to let it all go and just be, Scott. Just *be*. Without comparing yourself to anyone.'

'I've given up comparing myself, Kate.' Scott took a deep, visible breath. 'Number two is fine with me.'

Heart. Breaking.

'You're not number two. Not with me, Scott.'

'Not yet. But give it time. Someone else will come along. Someone older, like that Phillip guy. Someone smarter, like Hugo. Someone not as stitched-up and closed-off and conservative, like Brodie. That's why you danced with him. Why you went sailing with him. I'll bet you even told him about your custody case.'

She was silent.

'Did you, Kate?' he asked, and she heard the edge of danger in his voice.

'I don't talk about my cases. Not in…in detail.'

'Obfuscation? How very…*legal*.' He shook his head, disgusted.

'You sound like my mother. She really would like you, Scott.'

'Did you tell him, Kate? It's a simple question—one of those simple questions you say you don't have a problem with.'

She took a quick breath. 'Then, yes. That's the answer. I did. I told him.'

Scott's hand fisted, banged on the table, and Kate flinched.

'Why?' The word shot out like a bullet.

'Because he asked. As a friend.'

'I can't *believe* this.' Scott shot to his feet, paced away, then back. 'What the hell am *I*, Kate? I've been trying to talk to you about it for a week.'

He banged both fists on the table this time.

'Tell *me*!' Another bang. 'Tell *me*, Kate, dammit!'

Kate's heart had jumped right into her throat as his fists hit the table, and for a moment all she could do was stare at him. He looked a heartbeat away from breathing fire.

Out of control—at last.

And now she had to find words, when all she wanted to do was fling herself at him and wrap herself around him and beg him to let her love him, to love her back.

She realised she'd left it too long to speak when, cursing, Scott started to pace away again. One step...two.

'Wait,' she said, standing, grabbing his swinging arm so fast her chair toppled backwards. 'I'll tell you.'

He was shaking his head as he turned, wrenched his arm free. 'Don't bother, Kate. Just...just *don't*. It's too damned late.'

'I'm representing the father,' she rushed out. 'Who's been sitting on the sidelines going slowly out of his mind while his ex-wife's new boyfriend slaps his three-year-old son around. Something he's reported over and over and over. But nobody believes him. Because there's been enough mud slung to cast all sorts of doubts about him. His little boy screams and begs every time he has to go back to his mother after a scheduled visit.'

Kate's breaths were heaving in and out and she'd started to shake with the fury of it.

'My client ended up so desperate he kidnapped his own

child to protect him. And what did he get for caring like that? No more visits. At all. That's what.'

Her throat was clogged and swollen. The injustice of it was raging out of her, even though she'd won. Why? *Why* did it still get to her? No answer—it just did. And it was all too much. The case…Scott…her damned life.

'So you want to know why I didn't tell you, Scott?' she asked as the tears started. 'Because you didn't sign up for deep and meaningful, remember? And that's deep and meaningful to me. I needed you. But how could I tell you? What could I say? When you said—made it clear— Oh, God. I can't. I…can't. I…'

But she couldn't go on. She was choking on tears. And suddenly she gave in to them, sobbing into her hands.

And then she was in Scott's arms, held tightly against his chest. 'Shh, shh, Kate…I'm here.'

'No, Scott, you're not,' she sobbed into his shoulder. 'You're not here. Your body's here—that's all. Just your body.'

She tried to pull away but Scott held on. 'I'm not letting you go, Kate, so stop struggling.'

'And if I do? If I stop struggling?' She looked up at him. 'Then what? You'll ask me to spit out a few legal terms and take me to bed?'

'Yes,' he said simply.

'That's not enough,' she cried, and buried her face in his shoulder again. 'I want more.'

'So do I. That's why we're rolling it over.'

'No, Scott, we're not.'

'You just said you wanted more.'

'Not more sex! More…*more*.'

'I don't— I don't—'

'No, you *don't*,' she cut in, half-despair, half-rage, as she pulled out of his arms. 'That's the problem. Well, I'm not hanging in limbo any more, like a suspended piñata, waiting to have the crap beaten out of me.'

'A piña—?' He stopped. Incredulous. 'I'm not beating anything out of you. I would never hurt you.'

'Oh, you're hurting me, all right.'

'I'm *not* hurting you,' Scott said furiously. 'I *won't* hurt you. You won't hurt *me*. That's the whole point!'

'And I'm telling you—you *are* hurting me. Because I love you. And you don't love me back.'

The shock of it was plain on his face. 'You don't love me. Kate, you *know* you don't.' Pleading, almost. 'You can't. You don't want love.'

She laughed, shrugged, helpless.

Waves of panic were emanating from Scott. 'You said you'd never give someone that kind of power over you.'

'Except that now I would give it to you.'

'Cynical. We're both cynical. It's what made us perfect. *Makes* us perfect.'

'I'm *not* cynical, Scott. Or if I am it doesn't last—not if I have someone…' she swallowed '…someone who'll say to me, "Shh, I'm here", like you just did. Putting things right for people is what I do, what I *want* to do, even if sometimes it gets too much. And perfect…? I don't want to be perfect. And I don't want you to be perfect either. I want to be *im*-perfect—with you. I want children who are perfect or im-perfect—who are *anything* as long as they're yours. And I want to say to *you, Shh, I'm here*, when things get too much for you. Because I'm in love with you. And I would do any-thing—*anything*—for you to love me.'

His eyes were wild. 'I…can't do this.'

'Why not?'

'I don't. Do this.'

'You loved Chantal. Why can't you love me?'

'I didn't love Chantal, Kate. And I don't blame her for choosing Brodie. I never did. Anyone would choose him.'

'Not me. Because I chose you. I'm *choosing* you. No—it wasn't even a choice. It just happened. Love. I didn't even know I was waiting for it. But I was. I was waiting for the right man to come along. Then there you were. And suddenly you were mine. The perfect imperfect man. The right man for me. Uptight…beer not cocktails…hell, no, to dancing…sport and poker games…with a kitten on your backside…wearing a blue tux and driving a red Mini…baking for two little girls. How could I *not* love you? And now, Scott, I want us to just…just *be*.'

He was shaking his head. His face was white, stark fear in his eyes. 'I'm not the right guy for anyone, Kate. I'm the "friends with benefits" guy, with a bulging black book. I've never had a relationship—don't you see? *Never!* And there's a reason for that—because I know what I'm good at. Sex—no strings. My speciality. I've got more tail than I know what to do with. That's me. And I'm fine with that.'

It was like a punch direct to Kate's heart, killing it—that was how it felt. As if her heart was dead. A swollen lump she wished she could rip out of her chest.

'T-T-Tail?' Kate stammered over the word, her teeth chattering with reaction.

He looked at her, all hard-eyed. 'Tail,' he repeated.

God, the ache of it. Crushing. Ravaging. 'So here I am, opening myself to you, telling you I would move heaven and hell and everything in between—*everything*—to have you—*you*, Scott. Not Brodie, not Hugo, not Phillip, but *you*. And your response is to tell me I'm a piece of *tail*?'

He stood there like a block of granite, silent.

'Right,' she said, and swallowed. 'Right.' She looked blindly around, head spinning. 'Right.' Was the blood draining out of her? That was what it felt like. 'Saturday is the twenty-eighth of February. End of contract. We've had one session this week—Sunday. And we have tonight. We'll make this the last one, because I'm not inclined to negotiate any extras for the week. *Cadit quaestio*—a settlement for our dispute has been reached. Sex—once more—and the issue is resolved.'

'It's not resolved.'

Agony twisted through her. He didn't love her, but he wouldn't let her go either. 'What more do you want from me?'

'I want… I want…' His hands were diving into his hair again. But no more words emerged.

Kate took an unsteady breath. 'Well, given everything you've just said to me, and all the things you can't seem to say, I finally know what *I* want. I want out. I'm saying no to the rollover option. No to everything.'

'You can't do that.'

'Now, you see, you should have read the contract when I told you to. Because I *can* do that. I *am* doing that. I'm not going to turn into one of those bitter people I see in court— hating you, trying to punish you because you don't love me or need me the way I love and need you. If you don't love me then I don't want you.'

'You do want me. I know you do.'

Kate started removing her clothes.

'What the hell—? Kate, what are you doing?'

'Getting undressed.' She was down to her underwear in record time. 'I'm taking back my "Hugo" and we're restarting Play Time. As I recall, it was a dining experience you offered me—you bent the fifty-fifty rule to get it…clever you. So I'll get on top of the dining table, you can put those whoopie pies all over me, and then—'

But whatever she'd been about to say was whoomped out of her as Scott grabbed her by the arms. 'You're not lying on top of anything except my bed.'

She greeted that with a nice, brittle laugh. 'How conservative of you.'

'Yes, I *am* conservative. And I'm over all this Play Time stuff. I don't want you on your knees in alleys, or stripping for me like a hooker, or blindfolding me like we're in a B&D room, or any other kooky stuff.'

'That's exactly what you wanted—why do you think I was giving it to you?'

'Well, I don't want it now. Got it, Kate?' He shook her, once. 'Got it? I. Just. Want. You. As agreed. In bed. Okay?'

'As agreed,' she repeated. And the tears came. 'No, Scott, it's not okay.'

'Why not? Why *not*, dammit?'

'Because I love you. And loving you hurts like hell.'

He let her go, stepped back as though she'd struck him.

'Come on, Scott. Look on the bright side. You never liked all those rules. Anais is going to make you a much more *beneficial* friend.'

'I don't want Anais.'

'And after tonight I won't want *you*. So here I am, offering you one last time. Take it…or leave it.'

'They're the only two options?'

'Yes.'

'Then I'm taking it. Get on the table, Kate. Let's say goodbye in style.'

CHAPTER NINETEEN

SCOTT KNEW HE would never forget the sight of Kate lying on his dining table, letting him take her as tears leaked from the corners of her eyes.

He'd been so sure she would stop crying. That he could *make* her stop crying with the power of his depthless passion for her. But even as she'd succumbed to his body, as she'd soared with him into orgasm, her tears had kept coming... slow and silent.

Scott had been frantic. Scooping her off the table afterwards into his arms, holding her against his shaking body.

Wordless, she'd tried to leave. But he'd whispered that he wanted more, that he *needed* more. So she'd let him carry her upstairs to his bed. He'd kissed her for what felt like forever. But the tears had just kept coming. And even hating himself for her pain and his own desperation, he hadn't been able to let her go.

He'd watched her as she slept. The frown on her face. The tear tracks. The divine mouth, swollen from the way he'd devoured her.

She hadn't spoken one word to him—not since that last, 'Take it...or leave it.'

And he'd taken it, all right. Taken, taken, *taken*. Hoping, selfishly, to sate himself at last. Hoping he would wake up and not want her any more. Hoping he'd be able to let her go in the morning.

But when he'd woken she was already gone and he'd had no choice to make; she'd made the choice for both of them.

He hated his bed—because she wasn't in it.

So he went downstairs.

Where he decided he hated his house—because she wasn't there.

In the dining room were the girls' glittery boxes, waiting to be filled with whoopie pies. But the whoopie pies were nothing but a heap of broken biscuit and smeared cream on the floor, surrounded by shards of shattered plate. The plate he'd shoved off the table in his urgency to get to Kate.

As he looked at the mess and remembered how joyful he'd been, waiting for Kate to arrive, it hit him that what he hated most of all was his *life*—because she'd walked out of it.

And ringing in his ears, over and over, were her words. *'I would move heaven and hell to have you.'*

That was just so…*her*. Direct. Laying the argument out. Fighting to win. The way she always fought. To the death. To win the prize.

To win…the prize…

His breath hitched as he repeated that in his head. *Fighting to win the prize.*

The prize—*her* prize—was…him.

His heart started to thump. Loud, heavy, dull.

Why was he so scared about being her prize when she was everything that was wonderful? When *she* wasn't scared to claim *him* even though he wasn't anything wonderful at all?

But wasn't that exactly it? That time on her terrace, when they'd talked about love, she'd said that real love—of *any* kind—gloried especially in a person's flaws. She'd told him last night that she wanted to be imperfect…with him. She wanted them to just…*be*.

She knew everything. Chantal, Brodie, Hugo, his parents. Knew about all the times he'd lost. Had been with him when he'd finally won. She'd seen the very worst of him—because, God, he'd shown it to her—and she loved him anyway. He didn't have to be perfect. He just had to…*be*.

Eyes stinging.

She'd said she would move heaven and hell to have him. Chest aching.

That had to make him the best man in the world. Not second-best—*the* best.

Sweat ran down his back.

There might be smarter men, funnier men, better-looking men, more successful men, easier men—but not for Kate.

Breaths coming short and hard.

She would move heaven and freaking *hell* for him.

Whole body throbbing.

Exactly what he would do for her. Move heaven and hell.

Because she was his. Only his. And he wanted, at last, to reach for the prize, to claim the prize for himself—the only prize worth having. *Kate.*

The simplicity of that, the peace of it, burst in his head and dazzled him—but then the enormity of what he'd done to her, what he'd said, hit him and he staggered, grabbing for the closest chair.

Was it even possible to fix what he'd done?

Terrified, he grabbed his phone, called her mobile.

No answer.

Called her office.

Got Deb. Who had only two words for him: *'Drop dead!'*

He emailed Kate. Texted. Called her again.

He risked the wrath of Deb and called her again. *Three* words this time: *'Drop dead, arsehole.'*

So he tracked down Shay, because for sure Kate would have told her sister—she was a Cleary, not a Knight, and they were close—and maybe he could grovel by proxy.

And, yep—she'd told her sister, all right.

Dropping dead would have been a kindness compared to what Shay told him to do to himself, with a casual reference to Gus and Aristotle throwing knives at his corpse wrapped around a collection of four-letter words. She followed that up by telling him the most diabolical thing he could possibly hear. That Kate had never been in love before—but she was a Cleary, so that wouldn't stop her from ripping the love out of her heart and stomping it to a violent death. The Cleary way: fight like the devil—but when you lose, move on. No second chances. No going back.

Shaken, Scott hung up and did the manly thing.

He called Brodie and suggested they get drunk.

It was only beer number one but Scott didn't mince his words. There was no time to wait for the anaesthetising effects of booze. No time for tiptoeing.

'I'm in trouble,' he said.

Brodie took that with equanimity. 'I think what you mean is *I'm in love.*'

'Yep,' Scott said, and swallowed a mouthful of beer.

Brodie took his own long, thoughtful sip. 'I don't see the problem—unless she doesn't love you back.'

'She said she does.'

'And the problem, therefore, is…?'

'I told her I had more tail than I knew what to do with.' He grimaced. 'And that that was how I wanted it to stay.'

Brodie said an enlightening, 'Aha…'

'Well?' Scott demanded belligerently.

'Well, basically…' Pause for a swig of beer. 'You are an idiot.'

'Yeah, but what do I *do*?'

'Call her.'

'Tried. All day. Tried everyone. Her…her office…her sister. Her assistant told me to drop dead. And I won't tell you what her sister told me to do with myself because it's anatomically impossible but will still make your eyes water. I tried Willa. Then Amy. Just subtly, to see if they knew where she was going to be tonight. At least they don't seem to have any idea there was anything between us, so I haven't ruined *that* for her.'

There was a moment of stunned silence, and then Brodie hooted out a laugh. 'Are you *kidding* me? Nobody who saw you kiss Kate on that dance floor is in any doubt that you're a goner. The *bartender* knew, you moron.'

'Well, why didn't *I* know?'

'Idiot, remember?'

'So what the hell am I going to do?'

Long, thoughtful pause. 'Scott, I'm going to share something with you, even though you don't deserve it—you big clunk. Four words: *From Here to Eternity*.'

'Huh?'

'That night at the bar, before we got there, the girls were talking about their idea of romantic moments.'

'And...*what*?'

'Four scenarios were mentioned. One was Willa's—so let's discount that, because it was something financial.'

'Yep, that's Willa.'

'Then there was one about rose petals being strewn around the bedroom.'

Scott snorted out a laugh. 'God!'

'Yep. You wouldn't say *that* was Kate, would you?'

'Er—no!'

'What about a knight on a white charger?'

'What the—? I mean— *What*?' Scott burst out laughing.

'Not Kate?' Brodie asked, his mouth twisting.

'Hell, I hope not.'

'Sure?'

Scott shook his head. Definitive. 'No—that's not her.'

Brodie gave him a sympathetic look. 'Then I'm pegging her for *From Here to Eternity*.'

'What the hell *is* that?'

'A movie.'

'About what?'

'How the hell would I know? It's got to be a chick flick. I mean, come on—*eternity*? But I'm guessing there's a clue in that movie.'

'How's that going to help me?'

'Well, dropkick, I'm going to download the movie and we're going to watch it together. And—sidebar conversation—you are *so* going to owe me for this!'

'Okay, okay—I'll owe you. But what exactly are we going to do *after* we watch it?'

'I don't know—not yet. Which is why we're watching it in the first place. To figure out what her most romantic moment is. And then, mate, you're going to *give* her that moment—because words are not going to be enough. Action is what's needed.'

Two hours later—mid-bite of a slice of seafood pizza—Brodie paused the film. 'And there you have it,' he said.

'Have what?' Scott asked warily.

'That's the scene.'

'That? I mean...*that*? Seriously?'

Brodie replayed it. Nodded, very sure of himself. 'That. Believe me. I know women, and that's it.'

'Looks...sandy...'

'Suck it up, buddy. Suck. It. Up.'

'I can tell you right now I am *not* writhing around in the surf on Bondi Beach surrounded by a thousand people.'

'If that's what she wants that's what you're going to do.'

'Aw, hell...'

Brodie laughed. 'I'm just messing with your head, Knight. Nothing that public will be required. I have a friend down the coast who, as it happens, lives near a beach that is chronically deserted.'

'And just *how* am I going to get Kate to drive for hours along the coastline with me when I can't even get her to pick up the phone?'

Brodie held up a hand for silence. Grabbed his phone off the coffee table. Dialled. Then, 'Kate?'

Scott leapt off the couch, waving his hands like a madman and trying to grab the phone out of Brodie's hand.

Brodie punched him in the arm. 'Nope—haven't seen him.' Lying without compunction. 'Why?'

Scott made another mad grab—got another punch.

'No,' Brodie said, holding Scott off with a hand on his

forehead. 'I just wanted to offer you another sailing lesson on Saturday.'

Pause while Scott almost exploded—but in silence.

'Great,' Brodie said into the phone. 'Eight o'clock. See you then.'

Brodie disconnected and turned to Scott, grinning.

'*I* want to teach her how to sail,' Scott said.

'So do it.'

'Do it *when*, *genius*?'

'After the beach clinch. I'm going to drop Kate off at a particular inlet down the coast on Saturday, just after lunch. You—having bought a neat little yacht I happen to know is for sale—will have sailed down there and will be waiting to drive her to that deserted beach.'

'If I sail down there I won't have a car.'

'So *hire* one!'

'And then what?'

'And *then* you will roll around like a dumbass in the surf with her.'

'And…?'

'And you will sail her back to Sydney, teaching her the way you should have offered the first time she mentioned sailing to you. Honestly—do I have to do *everything* for you?'

Scott stared at Brodie. A grin started working its way across his face as he picked up a piece of pizza. 'I should have known a guy who'd order a seafood pizza would know all about girly stuff,' he said. 'Pepperoni is where it's at, mate. *Pepperoni*.'

'Shove your pepperoni where the sun doesn't shine, *mate*— and get me another beer.'

Scott laughed, and started to get off the couch to go to the fridge.

But Brodie stopped him, one hand on his forearm. 'You're it for her, you know? Don't let that mangy brother of yours keep getting away with making you feel like second-best. Because he is *not* better than you.'

Scott gripped Brodie's hand where it rested on his arm. 'I know he's not. She wouldn't love me if he was.'

Brodie smiled. 'And neither would I.'

'Brode—mate—*please*!' Scott said.

'You are *so* uptight—I'm not at all sure I shouldn't try to cut you out with Red,' Brodie said.

'You can *try*,' Scott said, and then he laughed.

CHAPTER TWENTY

Kate couldn't drum up any enthusiasm for the sailing lesson, but she was waiting at the jetty on the dot of eight o'clock, with a fake smile worthy of Scott himself pasted on.

Because it wouldn't do for Brodie to report back to Scott that she was looking wan and miserable.

She climbed aboard and darted a look around the deck. Half expecting… Maybe hoping just a little…?

'He's not here, Kate,' Brodie said.

She looked at him as the hope died. 'You know?' Short, unhappy laugh. 'Of course you do. Best friends, right? You don't have to badger confidences out of him.'

'Are we going to talk about it?' Brodie asked.

'No,' Kate said, and heard the dangerous wobble in her voice.

'Okay, then.' He took her bag, stowed it. 'Remember I said we were sailing down the coast and going swimming when we got there?' He gestured to her long cotton pants, her long-sleeved T-shirt. 'You got your swimmers on under there?'

'Yes,' she said.

'Then we're off.'

Kate tried to recapture some of the joy of her first sailing lesson, but that sense of freedom, of escape, was elusive. She was just so…so heartbroken.

Nevertheless, she threw herself into it—and if Brodie was a little less didactic this time around she wasn't going to complain about getting special treatment. He was that kind of guy—the kind who read anguish and allowed for it. Not the kind to tell a girl she was a piece of tail…even if she *was*.

Hours passed, and Kate started to wonder if they were going to turn around any time soon—because at this rate they wouldn't make it back to Sydney before Sunday morning. But they finally stopped at a calm, protected inlet for lunch.

Slowly Kate started to relax. But with relaxation came those horrible, useless, helpless tears. She hurried over to the bow of the boat, away from the others, trying to stem the flow. But it was no use. They welled in her eyes, clogged the back of her nose. Thank heaven she was wearing sunglasses, so Brodie wouldn't see.

But almost before the thought had formed Brodie was there, standing just behind her. She knew it, but she couldn't turn. Just couldn't move. Because the tears were flowing freely.

'He's not good with words,' he said. 'Not the *important* words.'

Kate covered her face with her hands, dislodging her sunglasses.

Brodie turned her, took off her sunglasses, hugged her. 'At least he didn't punch you. That's what he did to me the first time I told him I loved him.'

Kate started laughing then—and it was the weirdest thing, mixing laughter with tears.

Brodie tilted her face up. 'You going to give him another chance?'

'No. That doesn't happen in my family.'

'Well, at least you gave him *one* chance, I guess,' Brodie said. 'It's more than his own family gave him.'

'Oh, God. Don't say that.'

'It's true. He needs a family, Kate. A new one. A *real* one.' She was crying again.

'And he's over there on the shore, waiting for you to be it.'

Kate, stunned, turned to look.

And there he was. Tall and bulky, in jeans and T-shirt and aviator sunglasses, hands jammed into his pockets. Waiting for her.

Waiting...for *her*...

But waiting for what?

Kate didn't even notice when Brodie took his arms from around her. Barely heard him call to one of the guys on the boat. Dinghy... Something about a dinghy...

Next thing she knew she and her bag were *in* the dinghy, heading towards the shore. Scott took off his sunglasses as she got closer, flinging them away as if he didn't care what happened to them.

And then she was there, and he was reaching for her, helping her out of the dinghy, holding out his hand for her bag, wrapping her in his arms, holding on to her, holding tight. It felt electric—like a massive, hungry jolt—so different from the calm comfort of Brodie's embrace.

And she knew it would always be like that with Scott. Because he was *it*. The only one for her. It was a thought that scared her so much she almost couldn't breathe. Because it meant that without him she would be alone—forever. And she didn't want to be alone any more.

But being alone was better than loving a man who didn't love her back.

She took a deep breath, pulled out of his arms. 'Scott, I meant what I said.'

'Kate, please—just bear with me, okay? You'll see.'

Without waiting for her to respond, he took her hand, led her away from the water, up to the road.

He opened the door of a nondescript car—where was his Mini?—and helped her in.

'Where are we going, Scott?' she asked tiredly as he got behind the wheel, started the car.

'Don't ask, Kate. I'll stuff it up if I talk.'

So Kate simply sat as Scott drove—a total mess, almost ill from the way her heart was hammering.

He parked, got out of the car and came around to her side to help her out. He took her in his arms again and she couldn't bring herself to pull away. She felt him shaking. Like a leaf.

'Scared, that's all,' he said with an embarrassed shrug as she looked up at him.

'Why?'

Short half-laugh. 'You'll see,' he said again, and led her off the road towards a patch of scrub.

Her eyes widened. 'In *there*?'

Scott winced. 'Yep. In there. God help us.'

He led the way in until the thick scrub morphed into sparsely vegetated dunes. She could hear the roar and rush of surf, and then it was there. A tiny jewel of a beach, waves breaking in a constant sucking stream.

'A surf beach?' she said, poised on top of a dune.

'Yeah, a surf beach,' he said, grimacing, and trudged with her down onto the sand.

'It's beautiful,' Kate said, trying to understand the grimace—trying to understand *something*. Anything. 'And not a soul here except for that one surfer. Amazing.'

'It's a local secret,' he said. 'And apparently a little dangerous for swimming.'

'So why are we here?'

Scott screwed his eyes shut and blushed. *'From Here to Eternity,'* he said.

Kate's mouth dropped open. It took her a moment to find her voice, but at least by the time she did Scott had opened his eyes.

'Is this a joke?' she asked icily.

'No.'

'Who told you?'

'Brodie.'

She sucked in a tortured breath—felt the heat rush along her cheekbones. 'And who told *him*?'

'He figured it out. Something Jessica said that night at Fox.'

'Jessica?' she said ominously.

But Scott wasn't listening. He looked a heartbeat away from a nervous breakdown.

'Well, Kate, we're here,' he said. 'Let's do it.'

He stripped down to a pair of well-worn board shorts—in

which he looked mouthwateringly good. And then he came to her, took her face in his hands. Licked slowly along one cheekbone, then along the other.

'I've wanted to do that for the longest time,' he said. 'You are so absolutely beautiful when you blush.'

'Scott, this is not going to work,' she said a little desperately, hanging on to her resolve by a thread. 'I told you. No rollover. I'm done.'

'It's not about the rollover and we're not leaving until we do it—so get your gear off.'

'That surfer—'

'I can handle one surfer.'

'But anyone could come past.'

'Yeah—I know. It's a bit like the night Officer Cleary frisked me in Ellington Lane.'

'That was different.'

'How so? Did you know we wouldn't be caught?'

'No, I didn't know. But it was dark and I…' She huffed out a breath, aggravated. 'Really, I just didn't care.'

'And there I was, thinking you were law-abiding!'

'I am. But I'm not conservative. And *you are*, Scott.'

He touched her hair. 'And yet here I am, trying to get you out of your clothes on a beach in broad daylight,' he said, and smiled—and his whole face lit up with it.

Her heart lurched. That smile. *Devastating.*

'Scott, don't do this to me,' she said shakily. 'Stop doing this to me.'

'I have to do it. Kate, please. You've got to let me. Just this one thing. For you. Please, Kate. Please let me.'

Kate looked into Scott's eyes—they were warm and serious and…and *desperate*. Looked at the waves. Back into Scott's eyes.

Why was she fighting it? The man she was in love with was offering to make her a gift of her ultimate fantasy. She'd be like Willa and Chantal—her most romantic moment would be real. And she could pretend, couldn't she, that it was love?

'All right,' she said, and wondered if he'd finally driven her mad as she stripped down to her one-piece black swimsuit.

Scott took her hand. Gave her a look redolent of bravery. 'Shall we?'

She nodded, but wondered if this memory—precious though it would be—was going to be worth it, given that every time it surfaced in the future her heart would break all over again.

Scott led her into the surf, just far enough for them to duck under the water and get wet.

'No further,' he said. 'I can feel the water tugging, and this is going to lose all its romance value if we get swept out to sea and either drown or get eaten by a shark.'

He pulled her into his arms.

'And in any case...' he said, backing her towards the shore. Backing her, backing her, backing her, and then dragging her to her knees, where the waves were breaking. 'This is the money shot, right?'

And with that, he eased her flat onto the sand, and then he was on top of her, kissing her as if he'd happily drown as long as his mouth was on hers.

The water surged over them. Receded, surged, receded. For the longest time they stayed there, waves breaking over them, Scott's mouth on hers, tongue thrusting, mirroring the breaking of the waves over their bodies. Over, over, over. Way longer than the scene in the movie.

Eventually he pulled back, just a fraction, smoothed her hair off her face, gazed down at her. And something was shining in his eyes that made her long to have him inside her. She wasn't supposed to want it any more—she was supposed to have ripped him from her heart—and yet she did want it...did want him. She ached with need.

A sudden strong wave took Kate unawares and she choked on sea water. Scott grabbed her hand, dragged her out of the wash and up the beach to dry land, where she dropped to the sand and rolled onto her back, spluttering, laughing, coughing, eyes streaming.

And despite the fact that she was half drowned, deranged, probably a little snotty, Scott dropped to his knees beside her and looked at her as though she were the most wondrous thing he'd ever seen.

He was smiling, and there were tears—*tears!*—in his eyes as he rolled with her on the sand until she was on top of him.

She snaked her fingers into his wet hair, wanting him so much she thought she might seriously burst with it.

He looked up at her, so serious. 'So, Kate, what's the Latin for *And so endeth the contract*?'

She froze. *And so endeth...?*

Oh. Ohhh. Her breath caught as the pain hit.

It all made sense. Today was the twenty-eighth of February. The last day of their contract. She'd given herself to him at his house on Tuesday, fulfilled the contract to the letter, but he had to wring that little bit extra out of her—even after breaking her heart. Probably thinking she'd let him get away with this latest manipulation because he was using her secret fantasy to do it. And who *wouldn't* want their ultimate Play Time, right?

Hating herself for letting him do this to her—hating *him*—Kate shoved herself off him, got to her feet, started pulling on clothes over the dampness and sand.

Scott had felt the change in Kate that split second before she'd rolled off him.

'Did I stuff it up?' he asked, getting to his feet. 'Because I thought… I mean I watched the movie… I…I thought that was…'

The words tapered off as Kate skewered him with a glare.

Was this the part where she told him he was too late? That she didn't love him any more? No, he couldn't face that. Didn't—*wouldn't*—believe it.

Scott started dressing, just to keep his hands occupied

while he waited for her to speak, to give him a clue about where he'd messed up. But she didn't speak and he couldn't take the silence.

'Are you going to tell me what I did wrong, Kate?'

'You know.'

'No, I don't.'

'The twenty-eighth of February,' she said coldly.

Scott looked at her blankly.

'February *twenty-eighth*!' she snapped. 'You couldn't resist having the last word, could you, Scott? One last Play Time—and using my deepest, most secret fantasy to do it. Good job. For someone who said he would never hurt me, you sure wield a sharp knife.'

What the hell—?

She picked up her bag. 'So when is Brodie coming back for me?'

'Brodie's on his way to Sydney,' Scott said. 'I'm taking you back.'

The blood drained out of Kate's face.

'What?' he asked urgently. 'What did I do?'

She laughed—and it wasn't the joyful laughter they'd shared in the waves. 'Today. Last day of the contract, right?'

'Yes…' Still bewildered.

'I've spent three days tearing you out of my heart, and thanks to your little stunt today all that work is lost. I'll have to start over.'

Scott's mouth went dry—a dryness that had nothing to do with the ton of salt that had swirled in and out of his mouth with all that sea water. 'I thought you wanted the contract to be over?'

'I did. But not like— Oh, just forget it.'

He grabbed her arm. 'No, tell me, Kate. If you don't tell me, how can I explain?'

She wrenched free. 'Under the terms of our contract you don't have to explain.'

'Dammit, Kate, I've had a gutful of the contract. It's over! *Over!*'

'It was over on Tuesday, but that wasn't good enough for you, was it? Because *I* decided that. I decided it out of love. But you had to control the ending—out of…of…*pique*! And so here you are, controlling it—like you've controlled everything since the moment we met.'

'That's *crap*, Kate. I've *never* been in control. Not from the first moment I saw you. I don't— I don't *want* to be in control with you. And that—' He shoved irritably at his hair. 'That is not an easy thing for me to admit.'

'Oh, you've been in the driver's seat all the way along. Running rings around me. Flouting the rules. Turning up any time you wanted. All those calculated kisses to get me to shut up when I asked you a personal question—when I *told* you kissing was dangerous.'

'You never told me that!'

'It was *implied*! Because it's obvious! To everyone except you. Kissing—no problem for Scott Knight, because Scott Knight doesn't care and Scott Knight doesn't feel.'

'But I did—I mean I *do*—'

'Shut up, Scott. Just *shut up*. Because I *do* feel. And every time you kissed me I felt more—and more and more. Wanted you more and more. But all you wanted was Play Time! So I gave that to you too, because I figured I could *sex* you into loving me. I would have done anything. *Anything!* But you wouldn't even let me protect myself by sticking to a few simple rules.'

'Kate, stop. I—'

'You know what's the stupidest thing of all? I started to think that maybe you were breaking all those rules because you didn't *want* the contract.'

'I didn't. I wanted—'

'I thought you just wanted to kiss me, see me, be with me—take it however it came. The more you broke the rules, the more I hoped. But you were breaking them because it was a game to you. *I* was a game.'

'No, that isn't—'

'And that last night—what you said to me. *Tail.* A piece of tail. That's what I was. *All* I was. All the way along. And you, with more tail than you know what to do with, could have anyone—so why me? Why did you still take and *take* from me that night? When you knew how…how painful it was for me to love you like I did? You knew I wanted to leave and you wouldn't let me go.'

'Okay, that's *enough*, Kate!' He grabbed her then, dragged her in. 'I didn't let you go because I couldn't. I can't, Kate. I *can't.*'

'But you will—because tomorrow is the first of March and we are done.' She jerked out of his arms. '*Done!* Do you get it? *A mensa et thoro*—legal separation without divorce.'

'Don't talk Latin to me now.'

'*Res judicata*—the final adjudication. No further appeals. Goodbye.'

Scott blanched. His shoulders were tight enough to snap his spine. Head drumming. Heart hammering. Hands clenching and unclenching.

'Except for one thing, Kate,' he said. 'You love me.'

'Well, you see, I'm going to let Phillip the barrister help me get over that. Tomorrow—the first of March—when there will be no possible suggestion that I am still under contract to you. Time for a *new* contract. This time I might even get the *friend* part of "friends with benefits". Someone who w-won't h-hurt me.'

'I won't hurt you.'

She turned away, breath hitching. 'You already have, Scott.'

'Then I'll make it up to you.'

'You can't. You wouldn't know how. Because you've never been hurt and you've never been in love.'

'I have been hurt. When you left me. When you wouldn't

speak to me. More hurt than I thought was even possible. And you're hurting me now. And I'm letting you because I deserve it. Hurt me all you want. Any way you want. But just don't leave me, Kate.'

He came up behind her.

'Because I *am* in love. Right now. With you. First love. Last love. All in one. I'm here with my heart bleeding, aching for you, so in love I can't even find the words to tell you how much.'

She turned slowly. 'No…' she breathed. 'You don't love me.'

'Kate, if you think *anyone* else, in their wildest dreams, could have got me to watch a damned chick flick, let alone re-enact a scene from one… Well, you're insane—that's all I'm saying.'

'That was Play Time.'

He glared at her. Shouted. 'Newsflash, Kate. I. Hate. Play. Time. *Hate* it. Got it?'

'Then why—'

'And if you think rolling around in the surf like a lunatic is my idea of a sexual fantasy, you are wide of the mark, my girl. I've got sand in every nook and cranny of my body and it's bloody uncomfortable. A piece of seaweed is sticking somewhere I don't even want to think about—it may require medical intervention to get it extricated. And it's driving me nuts. But you know what? I will go back and roll around in that surf until we shrivel into prunes—with salt water pouring out of my ears, and snot streaming out of my nose, and that surfer out there laughing himself into convulsions, if it's what you want. Hell, I'll take you to Hawaii and we'll try it on the original beach!'

'I didn't *ask* you to roll in the surf!' Kate shouted back.

'You didn't have to ask! I did it because I'm not good with words, so I had to *do* something. I watched that movie for you. I'm on this beach because I love you. I *love* you! And, so help me God, if you don't call that weasel Phillip and tell him to back the hell away and stay the hell away, I am going to *kidnap* you.'

'Kidnap me?' she sputtered.

'On the yacht I bought.'

'You bought a yacht?'

'And I bought *music*—so I can dance with you on it. And I'm going to teach you to sail, and take you to the Whitsundays, and…and… What's so funny?'

'You,' Kate said, and laughed so hard she dropped to her knees. 'The way you said "m-music". Like it was p-poison.'

'Kate,' he said dangerously, 'you *do* realise how many women would swoon to have me tell them I love them, right? But you're the only one I'm ever, *ever* going to say it to.'

'Egomaniac,' Kate said, and kept laughing.

'It's not funny.'

'No, it's not. It's a serious condition, egomania,' she said, and laughed again.

Pause. He was confused. But…hopeful.

'Is laughter…? Is it good under these circumstances?' he asked tentatively.

'Accedas ad curiam.'

'Yeah, smartarse—going to need a translation,' he said, but a smile had started to stretch his mouth and he could feel it—*feel* it!—in his eyes too.

'You may approach the court,' she said. 'That's all I will say for now. And, Scott—just so you know—I have sand in every nook and cranny too.'

'Well, I think I'm going to have to take a look at your crannies, in that case,' Scott said, and dropped to his knees beside her.

He kissed her, long and hard, until they were both breathless.

'Are you going to take me to see your yacht?'

'It's not a *yacht*—it's a Jeanneau 36. If you're going to be a sailor you need to know these things.'

'Does it have a name? Like…you know…a *real* name?'

'It does,' Scott said, and started laughing.

'Which is?'

'Which is…drumroll…*Scottsdale*.'

Kate started laughing again and it reminded Scott of that night—the awards dinner—when they'd laughed about Knightley and he'd wanted her more than he'd wanted to breathe. He should have known right then that she was meant to be his. That she *would* be his.

'Wait until Hugo hears I've copied *him* for once,' Scott said, and then he stopped. Cleared his throat. 'Kate, just one thing… About my family…'

'That would be me,' she said softly. 'Just me.'

'Oh, God, Kate, I love you,' he said, and pulled her down to lie with him on the sand again. 'But you have to know that I have a bit of a conservative streak, like all the Knights.'

'You don't say?'

'So…divorce parties, break-ups, custody battles… They don't apply to us.'

'Don't they?'

'Because Knights don't divorce. And I will not let you go.' He stopped to kiss her. 'If you try to end it I'll make your life hell. I will fight tooth and nail—move heaven and hell and everything, *everything*, in between—to keep you. Exactly the way *you* fight. To the death. So better not to go there. You get all freaked out when marriages end badly. We don't want you stressing.'

'No more stress. Got it. But…Scott? Was that a proposal? Because we're not exactly marriage-minded in my family.'

'But I am. And, sorry to break it to you, but I have to be married to the mother of my children—conservative, I'm telling you, I hope your mother is going to cope. And one more thing. You're not getting any younger, so we'll have to get cracking on the kid thing.'

With that, Kate pushed him away, got to her feet, ripped her T-shirt over her head. 'My *age*? Are you seriously going there? Because if you are we're going another round of *From Here to Eternity.*'

Scott didn't argue. He simply stood up and took off his clothes. And then he turned to Kate and held out his hand. 'Or, as we like to say in legal circles, *ad infinitum*,' he said. 'Which means—'

'Forever.'

And then Scott grinned. 'Okay, let's put on a show for the surfer dude, and see how much more sand we can pack into our nooks and crannies.'

* * * * *